Anonymous

Supreme Council of the Ancient and Accepted Scotch Rite of Freemasonry

in and for the sovereign and independent state of Louisiana, valley of New

Orleans

Anonymous

Supreme Council of the Ancient and Accepted Scotch Rite of Freemasonry
in and for the sovereign and independent state of Louisiana, valley of New Orleans

ISBN/EAN: 9783337411015

Printed in Europe, USA, Canada, Australia, Japan

Cover: Foto ©Andreas Hilbeck / pixelio.de

More available books at **www.hansebooks.com**

AD UNIVERSI TERRARUM ORBIS ARCHITECTI GLORIAM.

ORDO AB CHAO,

SUPREME COUNCIL

OF THE

ANCIENT AND ACCEPTED SCOTCH RITE OF FREEMASONRY,

IN AND FOR

THE SOVEREIGN AND INDEPENDENT STATE OF LOUISIANA,

VALLEY OF NEW ORLEANS.

NEW ORLEANS.

J. H. KEEFE & BRO., PRINTERS, 57 GRAVIER STREET.
1861.

T∴ T∴ G∴ O∴ T∴ G∴ A∴ O∴ T∴ U∴

A RITUAL OF THE ANCIENT AND ACCEPTED SCOTCH RITE OF FREEMASONRY.

FIRST DEGREE.

ENTERED APPRENTICE, ...E∴ A∴

OFFICERS,

1st.—VENERABLE MASTER. ....V∴ M∴

2d.—FIRST SURVEILLANT........ ....1st Surv∴

3d.—SECOND SURVEILLANT............... ... .2d Surv∴

4th.—ORATOR..... ....Or∴

5th.—SECRETARY........ ....Sec∴

6th.—TREASURER............. ....Treas∴

7th.—MASTER EXPERT ....M∴ E∴

8th.—MASTER OF CEREMONIES........ ....M∴ Cer∴

9th.—STANDARD BEARER............... ....Stand∴ B∴

10h.—INSIDE SENTINEL ....Ins∴ Sent∴

FIRST DEGREE.

OPENING OF THE LODGE.

(*The BB∴ being assembled in the Temple, the Ven∴ M∴. fills the vacancies of the absent officers and gives a rap with his gavel repeated by the two Surv∴.*)

VEN. M —Bro∴ 1st Surveillant, are you a Free-mason?

1st SURV.—My BB∴ recognize me as such.

VEN. M.—What is your first duty?

1st SURV.—To ascertain whether the Temple is well guarded outside.

VEN. M.—Please ascertain it, my brother.

1st SURV.—Bro∴ Inside Sentinel please ascertain whether the Temple is well guarded outside.

(*The Inside Sentinel raps...... ! ! ! which is answered by the Outside Sentinel.......! ! ! —The Inside Sentinel raps another time....... ! and the Outside Sentinel answers.......!— Then, after having opened the wicket and being aware that the Lodge may begin its works, the Inside Sentinel says :*)

INS. SENT.—Bro∴ 1st Surv∴, the Temple is well guarded outside.

1st SURV∴ *repeats :*—Ven∴ M∴, the Temple is well guarded outside.

VEN. M.—Bro∴ 1st Surv∴, what is your second duty when the Lodge opens in the Apprentice's Degree?

IST SURV.—To ascertain whether the persons present are Entered Apprentices and members of this Lodge.

VEN. M.—BB∴ 1st and 2nd Surveillants, please ascertain on your respective columns if all the BB∴ present are Entered Apprentices. Ascertain also that they are members of this Lodge.

(*The 1st and 2nd Surv∴, in succession give a rap with their gavel, saying:*)—To order! BB∴!

2d Surv.—(*Gives a rap with his gavel and says:*)—Bro∴ 1st Surv∴ the BB∴ on my column are Entered Apprentices; they are in order. They are also members of this Lodge.

1st Surv.— (*Gives a rap with his gavel and says:*)—Ven∴ M∴, the BB∴ on both columns are Entered Apprentices; they are in order. They are also members of this Lodge.

Ven. M.—The East is also in order.

Ven. M.—Bro∴ 1st Surv∴, where does our Bro∴ 2nd Surv∴ sit in the Temple?

1st Surv.—In the South.

Ven. M.—Bro∴ 2nd Surv∴, what are your duties in the South?

2nd Surv.—(*Giving a rap with his gavel, replies:*)—To assist our BB∴ in preserving a remembrance of the impressions and sensations of the First of Mankind, when he saw the sun in all its glory pass the meridian of the celestial canopy and thereby learned to divide the day and its occupations.

Ven. M.—Bro∴ 2nd Surv∴ where does our Brother 1st Surv∴ sit in the Temple?

2d Surv∴—In the West, Ven∴ M∴.

Ven. M.—Bro∴ 1st Surv∴, what are your duties in the West?

1st Surv.—To as ist our BB∴ in preserving the remembrance of the impressions and sensations which our First Parent must have experienced when he saw the sun descend below the western horizon, illuminating the sky with golden drapery, succeeded by twilight and the obscurity of darkness, when all animated creation seeks repose, thereby learning of God's design in giving us a period for meditation and rest.

Ven. M.—Bro∴ 1st Surveillant, where does the Ven∴ Master sit in the Temple?

1st Surv.—In the East, Venerable Master.

Ven. M.—What are his duties, there, Brother 1st Surveillant?

1st Surv —To instruct our Fraternity in preserving a remembrance of the divine instruction given to our First Parent when he saw the sun appear again in the East, teaching him the importance of measuring time, and of improving it with useful works and researches.

Ven. M.—Bro∴ 1st Surv∴, when do the Entered Apprentices open their works?

1st Surv.—At noon.

Ven. M.—What time is it, Bro∴ 1st Surveillant?

1st Surv.—It is high 12.

Ven. M.—Since it is high 12 and it is the hour chosen by Entered Apprentices to open their works, please BB∴ 1st and 2d Surv∴, announce to the members on your respective columns that it is my intention to begin the works of this R∴ L∴ in the Apprentice's Degree.

1st Surv.—BB∴ on the northern column, I inform you that the Ven∴ M∴ intends to open the works of this R∴ L∴ in the Apprentice's Degree.

2d Surv.—BB∴ on the southern column, I inform you that the Ven∴ M∴ intends to open the works of this R∴ L∴ in the Apprentice's Degree. (*The 2d Surv∴ raps a stroke with his gavel and says:*) Announced! Bro∴ 1st Surveillant.

1st Surv —(*Gives a rap with his gavel and says:*)— Announced, Ven∴ M∴

Ven. M.—(*Gives three raps with his gavel and says:*)— To order!

To the G∴ O∴ T∴ G∴ A∴ O∴ T∴ U∴, under the auspices of the Sup∴ Council of the 33d and last Degree of the Ancient and Accepted Scotch Rite of Freemasonry in and for the Sovereign and Independent State of Louisiana, and by virtue of the powers on me conferred by this R∴ L∴ (*name and number*), I do declare its works opened in the first degree.

Ven. M.—With me, brethren! (*All unite in giving the sign and battery*) Take your seats, the works of this Lodge are open.

Ven. M.—Bro∴ Secretary, please read the minutes of the last meeting. (*The Ven∴ M∴ gives a rap of the gavel, which is repeated by both Surv∴ and says:*) Attention, brethren!

(*After the reading, the Ven∴ M∴ gives a rap with his gavel, which is repeated by both Surv∴ and says:*)

Ven. M.—BB∴ 1st and 2d Surv∴ please inform the brethren on your respective columns that they are now invited to offer remarks concerning the correctness of the minutes.

(*Both Surv∴ repeat:*)

1st and 2d Surv.—Brethren of my column, you are invited to make remarks, if you have any, before the adoption of the minutes now read.

(*If the minutes need correction, the Secretary will immediately proceed to make them as directed by the V∴ M∴*

(*If no remarks are made, the 2d Surv∴ raps a stroke of his gavel and says:*)—Brother 1st Surv∴, silence prevails with the brethren on the southern column.

1st Surv.—(*Gives a rap with his gavel.*) Ven∴ M∴—

Silence prevails on both columns.

VEN. M.—Brother Orator please give us your conclusions.

ORATOR.—We conclude the minutes of the last meeting be approved.

VEN. M.—With me, BB.·., for the adoption of those minutes.

CLOSING.

VEN. M.—BB.·. 1st and 2nd Surv.·., please inform the brethren on your respective columns that we are now prepared to hear such remarks as they may please to offer with a view to the advancement of the interests of the Order in general, or of this Lodge in particular.

(*Both Surveillants repeat:*)

Brethren of my column, you are invited by our Ven.·. M.·. to present such suggestions as may to you appear proper for the advancement of the interests of the Order in general, or of this Lodge in particular.

(*If no Brother wishes to speak, the 2d Surv.·. gives a rap with his gavel, and says:*)—Brother 1st Surv.·., silence prevails on the southern column.

1st SURV.—(*Gives a rap with his gavel.*—Ven.·. M.·., silence prevails on both columns.

(*If there are any Visiting Brethren, the Venerable says:*)—BB.·. 1st and 2d Surv.·., please invite the brethren on your respective columns to join with us in complimenting our visiting brethren.

(*Both Surveillants repeat:*)—Brethren of this Resp.·. Lodge, the Ven.·. M.·. invites you to join with us in complimenting our visiting brethren.

2d SURV.—(*Gives a rap with his gavel and says:*)—

Announced! brother 1st Surveillant.

1st Surv.—(*Gives a rap with his gavel and says:*)—Announced! Venerable Master.

Ven. M.—To order, brethren!

(*All rise.—The Ven.·. M.·. then briefly thanks the Visitors for their assistance ; the members of the Lodge unite with the Ven.·. M.·. in giving the sign and battery as a compliment to the Visitors.—One of the Visitors will acknowledge the compliment, and then all present unite in giving the sign and battery.*)

Ven. M.—Brother 2d Surv.·., what is your age as an Entered Apprentice?

2d Surv.—Three years, answering the number of my travels for light, and symbolizing my ignorance as an Apprentice.

Ven. M.—What time is allotted for work to an Entered Apprentice?

2d Surv.—Eight hours from morning till mid-day, and eight hours from mid-day to mid-night, at which time the hours of rest begin.

Ven. M.—What time is it?

2d Surv.—It is midnight.

Ven. M.—Since it is midnight and it is the time chosen by Entered Apprentices to close their works, BB.·. 1st and 2d Surv.·., please invite the brethren on your respective columns to assist me in closing this Lodge in the Apprentice's Degree.

(*The 1st and 2d Surveillants repeats:*)—Brethren, of my column, the Ven.·. M.·. invites us to assist him in closing the works of this R.·. Lodge in the Apprentice's Degree.

(*The 2d Surv.·. then gives a rap with his gavel and says:*)—Announced, brother 1st Surveillant.

(*The 1st Surveillant raps a stroke with his gavel and says:*—Announced! Ven.·. Master.

VEN. M.—*Gives three raps, repeated by both Surveillants, and says:*—To order, brethren!

To the Glory of the G.·. A.·. O.·. T.·. U.·., under the auspices of the Supreme Council of the 33d and last Degree, of the Ancient and Accepted Scotch Rite of Freemasonry in and for the Sovereign and Independent State of Louisiana, and by virtue of the powers on me conferred, by this R.·. L.·., (*name and number*), I declare its works closed in the 1st Degree.

VEN. M.—With me, brethren, by the signs, battery and acclamations.

We will now retire in peace, but before parting we will renew our promise of secrecy regarding all which has transpired here,

(*All extend their right hand and arm, palm down and say:*)

—We promise.

INITIATION TO THE FIRST DEGREE.

THE SECRETARY will rise and proclaim, after receiving an intimation from the Ven.·. M.·. to that effect, as follows: The following named gentlemen, (giving their names,) having been duly presented and successfully balloted by this Lodge, are in attendance awaiting an initiation.

THE TREASURER.—The candidates named by our Bro.·. Secretary have our receipt in full for initiation fees, in accordance with the by-laws of this Lodge.

VEN. M.—Such being the case, we will proceed to the

initiation. Master Expert, you will see that the candidates are properly prepared for our presence.

" Master Expert leaves the Lodge in due form."

PREPARATION OF THE CANDIDATE.

The candidate will be brought to the Outside Sentinel rooms. (the anti-chamber.) by the Brother presenting him. The Master Expert having a black veil over his face will approach the candidate, tap him on the shoulder and say:—"I am your guide, follow me."—He leads him aside, blindfolds him thoroughly, conducts him around the anti-chamber, and, if possible, out of doors around the Lodge buildings.

On returning he will divest the candidate of his coat, vest, watch, money, knife, keys and all metallic substance which he may have about him; his left arm, breast and leg to the knee must be uncovered; he may wear a slipper on his left foot.

Thus prepared, the Expert will introduce the candidate to the chamber of reflection, and seat him at a table prepared for the purpose.—Relieving his eyes from the bandage he will place before him a paper, in the form of a triangle, upon which must be written the following questions:

1st. What does man owe to God?

2d. What does he owe to himself?

3d. What does he owe to his fellow-beings?

4th, What does he owe to his country?

5th. Make your last will and testament, (briefly).

This room must be a small closet without other openings than the door—ceiling and walls painted or hung in black. It must be a receptacle for every insignia of death.—It will contain a small deal table and stool.—The room will be lighted by a dim taper.—Upon the table will be placed an inkstand, a pen, a cup of water, a piece of stale bread, and a human skull. At one end of the table will stand a mounted human skeleton.—At the opposite side, upon the floor, will be a coffin. The candidate will be seated with his back to the door. The Expert will explain to the candidate that he is now in a proper place for silent meditation and self-examination, and that he will leave him alone for a short time in order that he may the better answer the questions propounded. The candidate will write his answers in a legible manner and affix thereto his signature.

OPENING OF THE INITIATION,

VEN, M.—Bro.·, Master of Ceremonies, you will please report if there are any visitors in the hall, and bring us a list of their names, surnames, with their degrees, and the Lodge and jurisdiction to which they severally belong.

The M.·, C.·. will bring in the "Visitors' Register" and present it to the V.·. M.·,—The visitors will be disposed of according to Masonic usages. A visitor whose standing is not vouched for by a Bro.·, known to the Lodge must be examined by a committee appointed by the V.·. M.·.

Visitors are introduced by the M.·. C.·, in the order of their degrees, beginning with the 1st. A graceful salutation will be extended to them by the Ven.·, Master, and the M,·. C.·. will show them seats according to the regalia with which they may be clothed.

A single rap from the gavel of the V.·. M.·. repeated by the Assistants, calls up the roder of Exercises.

VEN. M.—Brethren, we are about to initiate to the 1st

degree of Freemasonry the following named gentlemen, or Mr—— All the required forms have been observed in their presentation, the ballot has been passed for each and has on every occasion been clear.

Now if any one has objections to offer they are invited to speak freely.

The Lodge shall duly examine such objections as may be offered, and shall direct that the candidate be either received, rejected, or that his initiation be deferred for further consideration. No objections being presented the V∴ M∴ will proceed with the initiation.

VEN. M.—As you think we may now safely proceed with the initiation, let us unite in giving the sign of adhesion.

VEN. M.—Brother Expert will please bring us the result of the candidate's visit to the Chamber of Reflection.

Brother Expert brings in the papers, hands them to the M∴ C∴, who takes them to the East. The Ven∴ M∴ will read the answers in an audible voice.

VEN. M—You will see if the candidates are properly prepared to enter this Lodge. Tell them that the ordeal through which they will have to pass is of a solemn and serious nature, and that we expect from them due attention, courage and care in order that he may avoid stumbling in his way, and successfully reach the summit of the mount from which he is to discover the light in search of which he has come; put a cable tow around his neck and lead him to our door.

The Expert will cause the candidate to knock violently at the door.

The Inside Guardian who has had a care to keep the wicket opened, cries out in a terrified voice.—Brother 1st

Surveillant, there is an alarm at the door.

1st Surv.—Ven∴ M∴, there is an alarm at our door.

Ven. M.—Enquire, Bro∴, and see who is the daring and imprudent man who comes at this dread hour to disturb our works and mysteries·

1st Surv.—Goes to the wicket and calls out:—Who is the rash man who comes at this dread hour to dirturb our works and mysteries?

Bro. Expert.—It is a candidate who desires admission to the venerable and secret society of Freemasons.

1st Surv—Ven∴ M∴, it is a candidate who desires ad. mission to the venerable and secret society of Freemasons.

Ven. M.—(Giving a heavy rap with his gavel·)—BB∴. let us rise and unsheath our swords, there is a stranger at the door.

All rise and unsheath their swords, so as to be distinctly heard by the candidate·

Ven. M.—What means this unexpected call, and what is your design?

Bro. Expert.—To crave at your hand, the initiation of the candidate to our ancient mysteries·

Ven. M.—By what right does he expect to obtain that favor?

Bro. Expert —By being a man free born, of competent age, and under the tongue of good report.

Ven. M.—What is his name?

" " age?

" " religion?

" " civil status? (married or unmarried·)

" " profession?

" " native country?

" " present domicil?

The responses must be taken note of by the Secretary.

VEN. M.—Let him enter.

The Inside Sentinel awkwardly slams open both folds of the door; the brethren present make with their gavels or other instruments, a rustling noise like carpenters at work in their shops. The M∴ E∴ seizes the candidate by the nape of his neck, holding him by the left arm, leads him around the Lodge, carefully conducting him over such obstacles as may be placed in his way, conducts him on the false ladder, makes him jump down, takes him to the altar where the M∴ C∴ pricks him slightly with the point of the compasses on his bare breast.

VEN. M.—Stranger or Mr.——, what do you see? what do you feel?

The candidate answers.

VEN. M.—The partial state of nakedness in which all must be introduced to our mysteries, constitutes the first symbolical lesson, and personifies the primal state of man after his creation. Although surrounded with every element of comfort, he found himself with no other resource than that of his bodily strength and powers, which he did not know how to use, in consequence of his primitive ignorance. This is symbolized by the darkness to which you have submitted yourself. In that helpless condition he must have been a prey to great anxiety, and his loneliness and feebleness must have been oppressive.

The puncture which you have felt on your bare breast, is the symbol of those first sufferings of his mind, and of the loneliness which overshadowed his heart. The future and the object of his creation were inexplicable, and a source of great uneasiness. Many an idea, no doubt, arose in his mind suggesting what he might do to make his way through the immensity which had suddenly enrolled itself before him, in all the brilliant glory of the universe of the New Creation, but want of experience led him to uncertain views, and he found himself a slave, and bound down by his own perplexities in the abode of liberty which is symbolized by the cord, which appears to restrain you of the free use of your limbs, and keeps you defenceless in the hands of an unknown guide. In a word, your condition is intended to impress upon your mind the circumstance attending the introduction of man upon earth, his entrance to a new and untried existence, with a world to conquer and subdue. So with you.--You enter upon this new world, naked, blind, helpless, and chaos appears to reign supreme. Let your mind seek for light, truth and liberty in this new world, and it will surely come to you. We will proceed.

Is it of your own free will and accord, unactuated by motives of curiosity or self-aggrandisement, that you have asked to be initiated to the mysteries of this Ancient Institution.

CANDIDATE.—Yes.

VEN. M.—It behooves you then to give heed to the difficulties which will beset you on every side. The path of life is strewed with care and disappointment. Every step in knowledge, which leads to light, calls for labor So here, your every step will be attended with fatigues, difficulties and trials, not to say dangers, which will call for the exercise of patient endurance on your part, accompanied by a persevering effort and presence of mind.

Are you ready, calmly and steadily to encounter them?

CANDIDATE.—Yes.

VEN. M.—It being so, we now leave you for a short time

to commune with your own thoughts. Bro.·. Expert, take Mr.—— to the rough stone.

The Bro.·. Expert takes the candidate just without the door and causes him to sit upon the rough Ashlar, returns to the Lodge leaving the door ajar that the candidate may overhear what is said.

Feigned objections are now raised with reference to the candidate's initiation, either by the introduction of a letter of accusation, or by causing a brother, whose voice is unknown to the candidate to impugn his motives.

A discussion arises thereon.

VEN. M.—Bro.·. Expert, please bring the candidate into our presence.

When near the altar the Ven.·. M.·. says:

VEN. M.—Mr.—— It appears from what we have heard that like many a stranger to Freemasonry you have for some time entertained erroneous notions concerning the institution. Like all institutions, whether sacred or profane, it has not escaped the tongue of envy, jealousy and all uncharitableness. It has been said by thoughtless persons that our mysteries are but as childish plays,....that we meet for the purpose of passing our leisure hours, in the revels of the banqueting hall, and that the tendency of the institution and the observance of its obligations and precepts, is to make us forgetful and negligent of the duties and love we owe to our families, and that we even propagate pernicious doctrines in matters of religion and politics. Without assuming to ourselves perfection in all things, we sincerely believe that you will soon discover that we are not amenable to these accusations; that they are unfounded and proceed from the envious and malicious.

On the contrary it is chief among our aims to attain to a

true knowledge of our duties to our God, to our country, and to our fellow-men.

Now if you have been prompted to approach our portals and to ask for initiation to the Ancient Mysteries of Free-masonry with no more praiseworthy motives than the gratification of a vain and idle curiosity, regardless of the consequences of imposing upon our kind indulgence, we would most earnestly advise you to withdraw, reminding you that in so doing, your trials will probably terminate in a manner quite different from what you may have been led to expect.

Has the judgment of this Lodge been guided by wisdom and· prudence, when a few moments since, its members exercised so much of confidence in your honor and upright-ness as to overlook the errors attributed to you? Can we rely upon the earnestness of your determination to become a faithful, honorable, upright Freemason, true to your God, to your country, and to your fellow-men?

Candidate.—Yes.

Ven. M —Bro·. Expert, let Mr.—— take a seat upon the bench of probation, while we devote ourselves to the solemn meditations incident to the great work before us.

A few moments of perfect silence prevail.

Ven. M.—BB.·., let us rise and pray.

Almighty Creator and Father of the Universe, we humbly bow our heads before Thee, acknowledging thine omnipotence and confessing our manifold weakness. Contain our hearts and minds, keep them within the bounds of equity, and be our light and guide in the path of Justice. Thou art one in all thy eternal perfections and self-distinctions· All powerful, all wise, all love, Thou livest by thyself and every being is indebted to Thee for existence; for we all live and move in Thee. Although invisible to all, Thou seest and rulest all. Pray, then, receive our adoration and vows. Protect and bless these peace workers who are here assembled in thy name, for the holy purpose of strengthening their minds against the suggestions of evil, of entertaining their hearts with the love of virtue, of learning how to rule according to Thy views and wishes, the passions with which Thou hast endowed them. We also beseech Thee in behalf of the stranger who desires to be initiated in our doctrines and mysteries. They lead to all that is true, beautiful and useful. May he with Thy aid prove himself worthy of the sublime order of Freemasonry of which Thou art the bountiful guide and master.

VEN. M.—In whom do you trust?

CANDIDATE.—In God.

VEN. M.—To trust in God is an act of belief, and whereas belief is necessarily based upon the feeling or reason, which determines it, we have to ask you this further question :— Why do you believe in God ?

After the candidate has answered as he may, the Ven∴ M∴ proceeds :

We believe that amidst the stupendous works of nature with which man found himself surrounded at his first appearance upon earth, an inspiration from above informed him of his physical and mental powers, placing him at the head of all animated creation, and that on viewing the splendor of the heavens above and the wonders of the earth beneath, he saw the handiwork of an Infinite, all wise and all beneficent Being, calling for his unbounded adoration and praise as the author and creator of all things—Believing himself to be the image and direct heir of his heavenly

Father. During the earlier generations of mankind, this active inspiration of the human heart existed in its greatest purity, giving to the soul of man exalted notions of infinite intelligence and of his immortality, leading him to a comfortable and ennobling communion through nature up to nature's God.

In subsequent ages man's heart became subject to evil passions, and his great source of comfort and of intelligence was obscured by the appalling darkness of all evil, and Paganism with its attendant degrading slavery succeeded to the knowledge of the true God, and man was not far removed from the beast of the forest.

In all ages, however, we find that there were a few wise and righteous men who strove with all their power to stem the mighty torrent of ignorance and of mental and political degradation. They had to contend against the mightiest for evil, among the religious and civil institutions of their time We find these wise men uniting in secret societies for the acquisition of strength for the preservation of a knowledge of the true God, for the restoration of man to his original, political and mental liberty and dignity of character. By the blessings of God they were powerfully instrumental in raising man to the high position in which we now find him.

We, as direct successors of those learned and philosophical societies, have a great work to do in the careful preservation of the wisdom and virtues of those great and learned founders of our ancient and honorable institution.

Mr—— will you please to tell us what you understand by the term Virtue?

The candidate gives his views thereon.

VEN. M.—In the same manner as there is in the universe a physical light which spreads its rays over the wonders of creation, in order that man may see, admire, and avail himself of them, so is there in every man an inward and intellectual light which diffuses itself in his mind, and shows him what he owes to God, to himself and to his fellow-beings.

A continued and sincere obedience to that inward inspiration is what we call Virtue, because it depends on us either to exercise or to refuse that obedience, and we can not lay claim to those divine qualities which distinguish man from all created beings, without a judicious and active exercise of reason in guiding us in our selection of good from evil.

Virtue is, therefore, that energy and tendency of the mind and feelings, which determines us in doing that which is good, beautiful and 'rue.

Mr.—— will you tell us what you understand by the term Vice.

CANDIDATE.—Gives his views upon the subject.

VEN. M.—Vice in our estimation is the reverse of Virtue, and results from a perverted judgment in the exercise of our power of selection, and leads us to adopt the evil rather than the good. We consider that man to be vicious, who instead of obeying the inward light or inspiration, which prompts him to all that is good, beautiful and true, gradually falls into an inclination to abuse his sensual powers and suppress his moral instinct without considering what is due to God, to himself and to mankind.

These three subjects, the ideas concerning God, Virtue and Vice, are at the foundation of the purest philosophy, comprise the whole of its moral teachings, and are susceptible of infinite development.

We had briefly to examine them with you, as preparatory

to your initiation, for we can receive no one without being well satisfied that his mind and heart are in a proper state gradually to attain to a participation in our mysteries and purposes. Know then the statutes and regulations of our society.

1st. You will be bound to secrecy regarding all that you may, at any time, see, hear and discover among us.

2d. It will be your duty to fraternize with all regular Freemasons throughout the world, and to help, according to the best of your knowledge and ability, all these among them who may need your advice or services in consequence of misfortune, sickness, persecution or other adversity.

3d. You will have to do all in your power to propagate among your acquaintances and in the world at large, the doctrines and principles of our Order, with a view to contribute to the Glory of the Grand Architect of the Universe, and to secure the progress of mankind in attaining to a larger and safer liberty both in Religion and Politics.

4th. You will have to obey not only the by-laws of this Lodge, but also the general statutes of the Ancient and Accepted Scotch Rite of Freemasonry, and the general regulations of the Supreme Council of that Rite in and for the Sovereign and Independent State of Louisiana.

Being now blindfolded you may hesitate in taking the required obligations, but we may assure you that in no particular will you find them at variance with your duties and obligations as a good man, a good son, a good father, a good brother, a good husband, a good friend, and a good citizen.

Are you ready to take the obligations?

Candiltae.—Yes.

Ven. M —(raps,) Rise, brethren, and unsheath your

swords and be witnesses of this solemn declaration.

Bro∴ Expert, please lead Mr.—— to the altar. The candidate will place his right hand upon the compasses and book,.and will repeat after Ven.∴ M.∴, as follows :

OBLIGATION.—In presence of the Grand Architect of the Universe, under the auspices of the Supreme Council of the Ancient and Accepted Scotch Rite of Freemasonry in and for the Sovereign and Independent State of Louisiana, and in presence of this assemblage of Freemasons of the same Rite, I, (*surname and name,*) of my own free will and accord do solemnly, and on my word of honor, promise always to hale and never to reveal any part of the secrets and mysteries of Freemasonry which may hereafter be intrusted to me, and never to speak of them except to a brother, or in a regularly constituted Lodge of the Rite ; and I would rather have my throat cut across and my tongue torn out by the roots, than to be untrue to this my promise.

VEN. M.—God help you in preserving your promise inviolate, and save you from that remorse of conscience which invariably attends a breach of honor and confidence. The consequences of a violation of this obligation will follow you like a weird phantom of darkness to your life's end.

Come up now, and partake of the cup from which we have all drank on the day of our initiation, and have no fears, for it is one of the most important and instructive trials through which we have to pass.

The Ven.∴ M.∴ resumes his seat. The Expert leads the candidate to the throne, and makes him taste of the bitter cup prepared for the occasion, and returns with him to a seat behind the altar.

VEN. M.—This bitter draught is symbolical of disappointments to which man is subject throughout his course of life. However richly, endowed with mental and physical powers, disappointment surely awaits us, and we are oppressed by the overthrow of our most sanguine expectations.

The extremity of joy sometimes leads us to the abyss of sorrow, and when we least expect it the most joyous laughter will be turned to bitter tears. It behooves us then to be at all times prepared to withstand disappointment under whatever form it may appear.

You have now several voyages to accomplish, are you prepared ?

CANDIDATE.—Yes,

VEN. M.—Guide this candidate on his first voyage.

The Expert seizes the candidate by the left arm, and with his right hand takes him by the nape of his neck, and makes him travel from South to East, from East to West, and from West to South, *three times.* Obstacles will be frequently placed in his path, and the brethren will make a noise, like carpenters at work, by hammering and pounding. At the conclusion of the voyage the Expert takes the candidate to the 2d Surv∴, makes him rap with his right hand, three times, upon the left shoulder of the 2d Surv∴.

The 2d Surv∴ places his left hand upon the candidate's right shoulder and strikes him slightly with his gavel upon the bare breast, and says :

2d SURV.—Who comes here ?

EXPERT.—A candidate who wishes to be initiated in our mysteries.

2d SURV.—By what right does he expect to attain that favor ?

EXPERT.—By being a man, free born, and under the

tongue of good report.

2d Serv —Who is to answer for him?

Expert.—I, his conductor.

2d Serv.—It being so, let him pass.

The Expert conducts him to his seat behind the altar.

2d Serv.—Ven.·. M.·., the first voyage is accomplished.

Ven. M.—Mr.—— what have you observed, heard and felt during this voyage?

Candidate.—Answers as he deems proper.

Ven. M.—This voyage is indicative of the confusion which prevails in men's mind on entering a new stage of existence, or upon a new subject of thought and investigation. Such is the position of a candidate here. He is entering a new world of thought, which will open up to him scenes both strange and new; unforeseen obstacles and remarkable phenomena will beset man's first steps in every new field of investigation, and his condition is likened to that of man when first placed upon earth, alone and unassisted, he was left to grope his way amid the darkness of the first night, his keen senses oppressed and overwhelmed with the alarming phenomena which appeared on every side. In this lone and dark condition his soul must have longed for knowledge and for light, and the future must have been for him a subject of exceeding anxiety. Your position is intended to inculcate the weakness of man, when alone and unassisted by light and knowledge he can scarcely expect to surmount the obstacles, and to progress without recourse to that great source of light and of knowledge, union and fellowship, with minds engaged in the same pursuits. Every step in knowledge gives us glimpses of undiscovered fields, shows man his own weakness, and brings him to a more patient and respectful consideration of the claims due to his fellow-beings.

You will now proceed upon your second voyage. Are you ready?

CANDIDATE.—Yes.

VEN. M.—Bro∴ Expert, please accompany Mr.—— on his second voyage.

The Expert takes the candidate by his right arm, conducts him around the Lodge, three times, from North to East, from East to South, from South to West, and each time he passes, he dips the candidate's left hand and arm into a basin of cold water standing near the door and the 1st Surveillant.

The BB∴ present make a noise with their swords as if engaged in combat or sword exercise.

At the conclusion of the voyage, the Expert causes the candidate to rap three times with his right hand upon the left shoulder of the 1st Surveillant. The 1st Surv∴ places his left hand upon the right shoulder of the candidate, striking him slightly upon the bare breast with his gavel, and says:

1st SURV.—Who comes here?

EXPERT.—A candidate who wishes to be initiated in our mysteries.

1st SURV∴—By what right does he expect to obtain that favor?

EXPERT.—By being a man, free born, and under the tongue of good report.

1st SURV.—Who is to answer for him?

EXPERT.—I, his conductor.

1st SURV.—It being so, let him pass.

Candidate resumes his position behind the altar.

1st SURV.—Ven∴, the second voyage is accomplished.

4

VEN. M.—Mr.—— what have you observed, heard and felt during this voyage?

CANDIDATE.—Answers as he thinks proper.

VEN. M.—This voyage is a symbol of the contentions in man's heart for the supremacy of the good and evil principles, teaching him that the character of the predominating principle within him is determined by his own will and choice, each carrying with it its own immediate consequences; that good actions lead to cheerful content, and that the prevalence of evil passions leads to bitter remorse. Our Supreme Architect and Grand Master, knowing man's weakness both in flesh and in spirit, and his tendency to depart from the paths of rectitude, taught him that his heart could be purified from its uncleanness by sincere repentance, and this idea is renewed and strengthened in our minds by the symbol of water, in the manner you have just experienced.

In the hands of the Almighty, water has ever been an instrument for effecting change in the physical condition of the earth, the rolling surges of the sea, the rushing mountain torrents, the gurgling brook, and the gentle shower, are each effective in producing change. As the Summer shower purifies the atmosphere and gives freshness and renewed energy to animal and vegetable life, making all nature rejoice in purity, so with the repentant tear over the corruptions of man's heart, it restores him to purity with his maker and with himself. Humanity is weak and not always well prepared to withstand temptation; hence it becomes us to extend an ample charity to the moral and intellectual weaknesses of our brethren, whilst our voices should be raised in stern denunciation of conduct, unbecoming a true Scotch Freemason and a gentleman.

There is, perhaps, no truer saying than that a man is known by the company he keeps. History and tradition teach us that the institution of Scotch Freemasonry has ever been distinguished for its ennobling and chastening influence over the human heart. We conceive that a true Freemasonic union is conducive to the highest degree of strength in the moral and intellectual world. In union we seek strength.

The two voyages which you have accomplished, are called; the first, the trial of Earth, the second, the trial of Water. There now remains one other, called the trial of Fire,

Are you ready to undertake it?

CANDIDATE.—Yes.

VEN. M.—Bro.·. Expert, please guide Mr.—— through the third voyage.

The Expert, standing on the left of the candidate, takes him by the nape of his neck, conducts him around the Lodge, three times, from North to West, to South and East. Three brethren will be stationed, one at the North-east, one at South-west, and one at the South-east with an apparatus for flashing chiropodium or other inflamable substance, and each time the candidate passes they will cause a flash before his face. The apparatus is shaped somewhat like a tobacco pipe, having a tube some four feet in length, and in the bowl a taper is so placed that the seed may be blown up to the flame.

When the candidate arrives for the last time at the East the Expert will make him rap three times with his right hand upon the left shoulder of the Ven.·. M.·., who taps the candidate with his gavel on his bare breast, and says :

VEN, M,—Who comes here?

Expert.—A candidate who wishes to be initiated in our mysteries.

Ven. M.—By what right does he expect to obtain that favor?

Expert.—By being a man of mature age, free born, and under the tongue of good report.

Ven. M —Who is to answer for him?

Expert.—I, his conductor.

Ven. M.—It being so, let him pass.

Candidate resumes his place behind the altar, and the 1st Surv.·. gives a rap.

1st Surv.—Ven.·. M.·., the third voyage is accomplished.

Ven. M.—Mr.—— what have you observed, heard and felt during this voyage?

Candidate answers.

Ven. M.—In the Ancient Phylosophies, Fire was considered strikingly emblematic of life renewed, and was an important symbol in the ancient mysteries. It being an effective agent in resolving matter into its elements, separating the pure from the worthless dross, so in the moral and intellectual world, the power of resolving and separating the pure from the impure, the good from the evil, has been symbolized by fire. It has ever been the high aim of this ancient institution to keep this fire burning fresh in man's heart, that at the last day he may rise, like the fabled Phœnix, pure part from the ashes of corruption. With the Ancients, Earth, Water, Fire and Air were considered as sacred elements, and candidates to mystic knowledge and light were obliged to pass through trials of each. Succeeding generations have, in a measure, modified those trials and entirely omitted the *trial of Air.* The candidate had to pass through long dark labyrinth, over dead men's bones and other terrifying symbols of earth—this the *trial of Earth.* He then arrived at an abyss of dark waters resounding with the roar of mighty and unseen cataracts. He had to swim across this abyss, and in this was the *trial of Water.* Then suddenly appeared to the candidate a long avenue of crackling, real flame, through which he had to pass and this the *trial of Fire.*

The wise men of the East deemed these rigid tests of moral and physical strength to be essential to the advancement of man in knowledge, and for admittance to the sacred Rites and Ceremonies. The perversion of the true objects of the institution of Freemasonry in the latter days, by the adoption of the English Rite, wherein Masonry has been made subservient to religious and political creeds, calls for strong and determined men, who will rally around the ancient landmarks, and rescue our venerable institution from the innovations and corruptions of men, who for ulterior purposes have divested the institution of almost every trace of its ancient grandeur. Notwithstanding the modifications which have been introduced in the severity of the trials to which candidates are subjected, we can safely say that no consequent weakness has been observed in the tie which binds the brotherhood in the Ancient and Accepted Scotch Rite, nor has any diminution occurred in their high sense of honor and of duty to God and man.

Invoking the names of those wise and great men, who have given us the most perfect of human institutions, we ask you if you are prepared to become their true disciple in the defence of Truth, Liberty and Justice, even to the exposure of your own liberty and life?

CANDIDATE.—Yes,

VEN. M.—Such being your resolution, you must give us

assurance of your determination in a manner more cogent than by mere words, even to the sealing of your averment by your own blood. Are you ready?

CANDIDATE.—Yes.

VEN. M.—From which part of your body shall blood be drawn?

Candidate answers.

VEN. M.—Our Bro.·. Surgeon, the sacrificer, will attend that the operation be skillfully performed.

This trial should be omitted unless it can be performed with skill. It is performed exactly as a surgeon prepares his patient for bleeding, the object being to make the candidate believe that he has been bled, without drawing blood. A cord is passed around the arm above the elbow, and the vein raised full.—A slight scratch conveys the idea of a cut, and the flowing of the blood must be imitated by the trickling of water from a tube, close the supposed wound.

VEN. M.—This free shedding of your blood is a symbol of self-sacrifice of individual interests and considerations, to the welfare and honor of the Fraternity, you are about entering, in sustaining the cause of truth and of justice, and is indicative of the universality and intimacy of the tie which binds all true Masons in the bonds of brotherhood.

Difference of nationality and language has been no barrier to a recognition of our brethren; for, our predecessors established words and signs, which have been adopted throughout the earth. At a later period cowans, eavesdroppers and bad men have in part divulged some of our secret modes of recognition, so that a new and infallible sign had to be adopted. This sign will remain with you throughout life, and be easily recognized by Freemasons in all places, and should you ever be untrue to your Masonic vows, it will corrode clean to your heart and prove to be a stigma rather than an honorable distinction. This hieroglyphic is indelibly impressed upon the candidate's left breast with a hot iron, without inflicting a serious wound. Are you ready to receive this honorable mark of distinction?

CANDIDATE.—Yes.

VEN. M.—Bro.·. Sacrificer, please exercise your skill and care.

The trial of the mark must be conducted with skill. A pan of burning coals will be brought near the candidate, and a brother will imitate the heating of a branding iron. The Expert will take a burning candle, extinguish the flame, and immediately press the heated wick end upon the candidate's breast as in the act of branding.

VEN. M.—The method of teaching by symbols is very ancient, and has received the sanction of the wisest and best men. The symbols we have given you, are full of instruction, and we have deemed it proper to allude to them only in general terms, merely designing to introduce you to a new field of study and of thought, believing that you will find your advantage in giving heed thereto.

The institution of Freemasonry has ever been the depository of liberal principles in regard to matters of government and of religion, and a staunch advocate of the rights and liberties of the people. It has, hence, occurred that it has frequently come in conflict with despotic government and with autocratic priestcraft, and has been unscrupulously persecuted by them· Even at this day it is viewed with great disfavor by those powers as interfering with what they are pleased to call their divine prerogatives.

We, in the United States of America, are not exempt

from the specious presumptions of despotism, and it behooves us to preserve untarnished the armor of our ancestors, that by the strength of our union we may the better defend the liberties of the people.

We now pass to another of our most important obligations, that of Charity.

Ancient and Accepted Scotch Masonry has no ambition to be considered a *charitable institution* in the modern acceptation of that term. In that regard we are widely different from those secret associations whose claim to public consideration is in the assistance they render to the unfortunate poor. However laudable alms giving may be, we are not prepared to accept it with them as a full and complete exercise of all our duties as conveyed in the word *Charity.*

Alms giving is not the full scope of Charity as taught in the old Freemasonic schools of Philosophy. The greatest of the divine virtues given to man is Charity. It is that great vital principle of Fraternity, of Equality, and of Liberty which prompts a man to love his neighbor as himself—It is humble, retiring, hath no shadow of envy, hatred, or malice—it is that love to mankind which prompts us to rush to the rescue of our brethren in adversity as well as to rejoice with them in their prosperity. In brief, this is the substance of all our teachings, and all else is but subsidiary.

Bro.˙. Expert, please conduct the candidate through the dark vault. Explain to him its secrets, and take him to the place where you first received him.

The Expert takes him out and causes him to walk about, until called for the ceremonies of St. John the Baptist's head.

The table with its platter, ax, and linen will be placed near the door. All lights extinguished except from the three tripods, arranged triangularly around the table. A brother will be placed under the table so that his head alone will appear above. The platter is made so as to fit around the neck. By inclining the head to one side, and giving the face a cadaverous appearance with powder or flour and by a proper adjustment of bloody linen, a perfect resemblance of a decapited head may be given. All the brethren present will arrange themselves in a semi-circle about the table facing the door, with swords presented. When the arrangements are completed, the candidate will be introduced, the spirits of wine in the tripods lighted, the swords pointing towards him. The Ven.∴ M∴. standing by the head, gives three raps with his gavel in such a manner that the Expert may let the bandage drop from the candidate's eyes at the last rap.

VEN. M —This, indeed, is a sad sight! However horrible it may appear, let no fears arise in your mind. The scene is in commemoration of the awful death of an honest man, John the Baptist, who preferred the torments of a dungeon, even an ignominious death, beheading, rather than betray Honor, Justice and Virtue. The records and traditions of the past give no intimation that John the Baptist was a Mason. The anniversary of his death occurring in the same day as an Ancient Masonic festival held in commemoration of an astronomical period, led to the commingling of the two.

The remarkable character of the man and of his mission as the Forerunner of the Great Teacher of Fraternity, of Equality, and of Liberty, and his adoption of a mystic ceremony as a prerequisite to initiation, to christianity, and

5

his honorable self-sacrifice to truth, made his character and his name preeminently worthy of commemoration by Free-masons. His life and death furnish us with a most re-markable instance of fidelity to honor and to truth, and his memorable example will be cherished by Masons throughout all times.

Bro.· Expert, you will please let the candidate resume his clothing and conduct him blindfolded into the Temple. (The Expert blindfolds him again and leads him out. The Lodge will now be put in order. The implements used in the trials placed out of sight. When called to order the candidate will be brought in.)

Ven. M.—(raps,) BB.·, let us rise and unsheath our swords.

Bro·. 1st Surv.··, you have been a witness of the firm-ness, patience, and attention with which this candidate has passed through the many trials, to which he has been sub-jected in accordance with the customs of this Ancient Fraternity, and the will of this Lodge. Do you think him worthy of being received among us?

1st Surv.—I think he is.

Ven. M.—(raps,) what do you ask for him?

·1st Surv.—Light·

Ven. M.—(raps,) What do you ask for him?

1st Surv —Light.

Ven. M.—(raps,) What do you ask for him?

1st Surv.—Light, and great light.

Ven. M.—Let there be light·

The Expert lets the bandage drop suddenly from his eyes. The BB.·. present extend the points of their swords towards him in sign of protection.

Ven. M.—Fear not those swords, they are in the hands

of friends, devoted brethren who with the vast army of Freemasons scattered over the earth, extend to you the hand of protection, of assistance, and of love.

Bro.·. M.·. C.·., please conduct our new friend to the altar, and we will constitute him App.·. Freemason, and an active member of this Respectable Lodge·

The Ven.·. M.·. goes to the altar, extends his sword over the candidate's head, holding a gavel in his right hand, and says :

" To the Glory of the Grand Architect of the Universe, under the auspices of the Supreme Council of the 33d Degree of the Ancient and Accepted Scotch Rite in and for the Sovereign and Independent State of Louisiana, and by virtue of the powers on me conferred by this R.·. Lodge, (name and number,) of the same Rite, I do hereby make and constitute you an Apprentice Freemason and an active member of this Lodge."

The Ven.·. M.·. gives, then, three raps with his gavel upon the blade of his sword, shakes hands with the candidate, and resumes his place in the East.

Ven. M.—Bro·. M.·. C.·., please conduct our new brother to the East for instruction.

The M.·. C.·. gives him a seat near the Secretary to the right of the throne. The Ven.·. M.·. approaches him and addresses him thus :

Ven. M.—As before remarked, time will permit us to give you only a general idea of the subjects offered for the study of the Entered Apprentice· On future occasions you will have them more fully illustrated, and be better prepared to understand.

When you were taking your obligations, your right hand was resting upon compasses.

As in the hands of the Architect, the compasses enable him to give those accurate proportions, which give beauty and stability to his work, so here is it an important and striking symbol of that even tenor of deportment and that true standard of rectitude, which should distinguish every Freemason. "It is ordained in the eternal constitution of things, that men of intemperate passions can not be free; they forge their own fetters." The compasses instruct us in the duty we owe to ourselves, teaching us so to circumscribe our passions and restrain our desires, that we may present a character just in all its proportions, marked for its beauty and stability. They are to us as the sun, giving us light to govern and guide ourselves.

This room with its appointments is a symbol of the universality of Masonry, is called a Lodge and represents the world. Here we have the illuminated East, the North-West and South being in darker colors.

The ceiling represents the celestial canopy.

Our Lodge is the world, signifying that in every clime the Mason may find a home, and in every land a brother.

We now invest you with the badge of an Entered Apprentice Mason. When you enter a Lodge, wear this white apron thus—(The Ven∴. M∴. ties the apron around the Apprentice's loins, turning up the flaps on the right side.) The whiteness of its color admonishes us to preserve that blameless Purity of life and conduct which alone can enable us to present ourselves in the consciousness of Purity before the Grand Master of the Universe.

The Ven∴. M∴. then presents him with a twenty-four inch gauge and a gavel, and says:

We now present you with the working tools of the Entered Apprentices.

This gauge is divided into twenty-four equal parts, emblematic of the divisions of the day into twenty-four hours, which being embraced in three equal parts, gives eight hours from East to West for labor, eight hours from South to West for the service of God and our worthy BB.·., and eight hours from West to East for meditation and rest.

The gavel, you are aware, is used with the gauge for adapting and preparing materials to the builders use ; so they admonish the Entered Apprentice to prepare his mind for the reception of the great truths which are hereafter to be unfolded to him, to lay the corner stone and foundation of his character in Virtue and Purity, that the superstructure may be alike honorable to himself and to the Fraternity.

When you wish to enter a Lodge, you will rap at the door thus, (shows him.) On being admitted, you will in advancing to the altar make three steps, each describing a square thus, (shows him,) you will then exhibit the sign, (shows him,) first to the East, then to the West, then to the South, and take a seat under the column designated B. Explains the initial B, gives him the Sacred Word and the manner of communicating it, and finally the grip and battery.

Bro.·. C.·., please conduct Bro.·., (name,) to the West that the 1st Surv.·. may examine him upon the secret instructions which we have given him.

The 1st Surv.·. examines him with regard to rapping at the door, the step, sign, word and battery.

1st SURV.—Ven.·. M.·., his instructions are correct.

VEN. M.—Bro.·. M.·. C.·., you will officially proclaim the initiation of Mr.—— (name,) to the first degree, as an Entered Apprentice, and an active member of (name of

Lodge and number,) of the Ancient and accepted Scotch Rite, inviting the Fraternity to receive him accordingly.

M∴ C∴ takes his position on the step, in the East, holding his sword in his right hand, fore arm extended horizontally, sword vertical, point up.

I do hereby proclaim that Mr.——, (name.) has been duly initiated to the first degree of the Ancient and Accepted Scotch Rite, and legally constituted an Entered Apprentice and an active member of, (Lodge, name and number,) and he will be received and honored accordingly.

Ven. M.—1st and 2d Surv∴, please announce to the BB∴ on your respective columns that our Bro∴ Orator will now favor us with a work in Freemasonic Architecture.

Lecture on the First Degree of Scotch Free masonry

Q.—Bro∴ 1st Surveillant, what is the tie by which we are united?

A.—Freemasonry

Q.—What is Freemasonry?

A.—Freemasonry is eminently a philosophical Institution, embracing within its scope the preservation of social, political and religious liberty, and generally, all subjects appertaining to the welfare of man, as an intellectual and social being

Q —Are you a Freemason?

A.—My brothers recognize me as such.

Q.—To what Rite do you belong?

A.—To the Ancient and Accepted Scotch Rite.

Q.—What do you understand by Rite?

A.—I understand by the word Rite, one of the different for ns through which Freemasonry is worked.

Q.—What do you understand by Scotch?

A.—This word merely indicates that a Freemason, Ramsey by name, journeyed from Scotland to France, where he worked several degrees of our Rite, and Freemasonry in order to honor him, called these degrees,

Scotch degrees or Scotch Freemasoury.

Q.—What do you understand by Ancient?

A.—I mean that our Rite, though divided into thirty-three degrees at a modern period, may be traced back to the remotest antiquity, as far its doctrines are concerned.

Q.—What do you understand by Accepted?

A.—I mean that all Freemasons, seeking in Freemasonry the triumph of Fraternity, Equality and Liberty among their fellow-beings, must accept and work our Rite, which is, in all its degrees, the illustration of the principles contained in these three words.

Q.—Why do you come in this Lodge?

A.—I come to learn my rights and my duties as man, as citizen and mason

Q.—Where have you been received Freemason?

A.—In the bosom of a just and perfect Lodge.

Q.—What is required to have a just and perfect Lodge?

A.—It is governed by three, lighted by five, and made just and perfect by seven.

Q.—Who are the three?

A.—The Ven.·. M.·. and the two Surveillants.

Q.—Who are the five?

A.—The Ven.·. M.·., the two Surv.·., the Orator and the Secretary, who are called the five lights of the Lodge.

Q.—Who are the seven?

A.—The five first officers and the active members of the Lodge.

Q.—How long have you been a Freemason?

A.—Since I received the light.

Q.—How shall I know you to be a Mason?

A.—By certain signs, by a word and by a grip.

Q —What are the signs?

A.—All right angles, horizontally and perpendicularly.

Q.—Give me the sign.

A.—(The sign is given)

Q.—What does it mean?

A.—That I should prefer to have my throat cut than ever betray the cause of Freemasonry, and to fail in the promises I have solemnly made in presence of my brethren.

Q.—Give the grip to M.·. Expert.

A.—(He gives the grip to M.˙. Expert who, being satisfied says : The grip is just and perfect.)

Q.—Give me the word.

A.—Ven.˙. M.˙., I do not know, being only an Apprentice Mason, how to read, how to write. All that I know is how to spell. Give me the first letter and I will give you the second.

Q.—Spell it and begin.

A.—(The word is then spelled.)

Q.—What is the form of a Lodge?

A.—An oblong square.

Q.—How long?

A.—From East to West.

Q.—How wide?

A.—Between North and South.

Q.—How high?

A.—From the surface of the earth to the highest heavens.

Q.—How deep?

A.—From the surface to the center.

Q.—What do these dimensions mean?

A.—They are symbols to indicate that Freemasonry being an universal institution, ought to be worked in all countries of the world.

Q.—What do you mean by the word Lodge?

A.—The Lodge is a secret place where Freemasons meet to perfect their works.

Q —Why do Freemasons meet in a secret place?

A.—In order not to be disturbed by the enemies of Fraternity, Equality and Liberty, and to better accomplish the great work of Freemasonry.

Q —What supports your Lodge?

A.—Three large columns or pillars.

Q.—What are their names?

A.—Wisdom, Strength and Beauty.

Q.—Why so?

A.—It is necessary there should be Wisdom to contrive, Strength to support, and Beauty to adorn all great and important undertakings, but more especially this of ours.

Q.—How were you introduced into the Lodge when you were initiated?

A.—By three great and distinct knocks at the door.

Q.—What do those three distinct knocks mean ?

A.—" Ask and it shall be given, seek and ye shall find, knock and it shall be opened unto you."

Q.—Did you receive what you asked ?

A.—I have received the Masonic light, which I asked.

Q.—Did you find what you sought ?

A.—I have found a society of Free men, who are now my brothers, and who promised me help and assistance during the course of my life.

Q.—Did they open unto you ?

A.—They have opened the doors of a temple where lies the Mason's secret which it is the duty of all Apprentice Masons to deserve.

Q.—Do you know that secret ?

A.—As Apprentice Mason, no. I have to ascend the last degree of Scotch Free Masonry, which is the thirtieth, and all that time I have to study with energy and perseverance.

Q.—How was you disposed of, after your introduction in this Temple.

H.—I was submitted to several physical and moral trials, and having sustained them to the satisfaction of Freemasons present, I was constituted Apprentice Mason.

Q.—Where does an Appprentice Mason sit in the Temple ?

A.—In the North.

Q.—Why ?

A.—Because the darkest part of the world being symbolically represented by the North, the Apprentice Mason sit temporarily there, with the hope of receiving more light in the mysteries and secrets of Freemasonry.

Q.—Where does our Bro.·. 2d Surv.·. sit in the Temple ?

A.—In the South, Ven.·. M.·.

Q.—What are his duties in the South ?

A.—To assist our BB.·. in preserving a remembrance of the impressions and sensations of the first of mankind, when he saw the sun in all its glory pass the meridian of the celestial canopy, and thereby learned to divide the day and its occupations.

Q.—Where does our Bro.·. 1st Surv.·. sit in the Temple ?

A.—In the West, Ven.·. M.·.

Q.—What are his duties in the West?

A·—To assist our BB.·. in preserving a remembrance of the impressions and sensations which our First Parent must have experienced when he saw the sun descending below the western horizon, illumining the sky with golden drapery, succeeded by twilight and the obscurity of darkness when all animated nature seeks repose, thereby learning of God's design in giving us a period for meditation and rest.

Q.—Where does the Ven.·. M.·. sit in the Temple?

A.—In the East, Ven.·. M.·.

Q.—What are his duties there?

A.—To instruct our Fraternity in preserving a remembrance of the divine instructions given to our First Parent when he saw the sun appear again in the East, teaching him the importance of measuring time and of improving it with useful works and secrecy.

Q.—What is your age as an Apprentice Mason?

A.—Three years.

SECOND DEGREE,

FELLOW CRAFT.

OPENING OF THE LODGE.

The Lodge must be opened in the First Degree, and then in the Second. The opening of the Second Degree is conducted in the same manner as the First, with the exception of the Sign and Battery.

When apprentices are to be initiated to this degree, the introductory ceremonies are the same as in the First Degree; such as the introduction of visitors, announcement of the object of the meeting, etc.

PREPERATION FOR INITIATION.

Upon a table, standing between the altar and the door, the following named instruments will be symmetrically arranged :

One twenty-four inch Guage;   *One Mallet;*
One pair of Compasses;   *One Chisel;*
One common flat Ruler;   *. One Ruler;*
One Trestle or tracing Board;   *One Square;*
One Plumb Line;   *One Lever;*
        And one Trowel.

The candidate must be divested of coat, vest and cravat, wearing slippers instead of shoes, and have a cord passed three times around his loins, with a knot in front, the two ends of the rope hanging to the ground; the apron worn as in the App.·. Degree; he will carry a common ruler upon his right shoulder.

INITIATION.

Ven. M.—Bro.·. M.·. C.·., please inform our Bro.·. Expert that we are ready to proceed.

(*The apprentice gives the rap of his degree at the door. The Inside Sentinel looks out at the wicket, and informs the 1st Surveillant that there is an App.·. at the door.*)

1st Surv.—(*Raps.*)V.·. M.·., there is an App.·. rapping at the door.

Ven. M.—What are his wishes?

1st Surv.—(*Enquires and says:*—The apprentice is in charge of our Bro.·. Expert, and says that he has served his full time and wishes to be passed to the Fellow Craft Degree.

Ven. M.—What is his name?—His status?—His Masonic age?—How does he expect to be passed to the fellow craft degree?

Bro. Expert.—(*Through the wicket.*)Because he has served his full time as an App.·. with honor to himself and to his profession, and bears a good character for honor and probity with us and in the world.

Ven. M.—It being so, let him enter.

The Expert conducts him to the front of the table, where he gives the App.·. sign and remains standing.

The Ven.·. M.·. interrogates him on the First Degree as

far as he deems proper, and proceeds with

INTRODUCTORY REMARKS.

The Degree to which you are now about to be passed is particularly to scientific investigations; and as the lessons in the 1st Deg.·. were principally directed to the moral culture of the heart, so here our attention is called to the development of the mind by an examination and prolonged study of the invariable truths of science, whereby we are enabled to contemplate with reverence and admiration the glorious works of creation, and attain to clear ideas of the perfections and infinite Wisdom of the Grand Architect of the Universe. In the earlier periods, learning was for the most part confined to the Magi, Druids, and Priests of Egypt, who lived in lonely habitations and in caverns, and devoted themselves to the study of sciences, and attained to great reputation also for purity of morals and knowledge of the science of government.

They communicate their knowledge only to the initiated, and by the use of symbols, unintelligible to all who had not received the sacred rites. Ignorance brooded over the land like the darkness of night, and could only be dissipated by the gradual diffusion of light in the minds prepared to receive it. The period of probation for an apprentice was rarely less than three years, during which period he was expected to preserve a clear and unblemished character, and to have devoted himself assiduously to the learning of his degree. As knowledge became more generally disseminated, this period has been greatly abridged, and is now limited only by the progress he has made in his masonic instructions.

We are pleased to notice in the present instance the

unanimity which prevails regarding your advancement to a higher degree. You will have noticed that in the apprentice's degree the candidate has three voyages to perform, corresponding to the age he must attain in that degree. So here you will have five voyages to accomplish, indicative of the age you must attain in this, before being raised to the Master's Degree.

You will now commence your voyages.

Bro.·. Expert, you will please conduct our Bro.·. App.· on his first voyage.

Candidate has a Mallet in his right hand, Chisel in his left hand, passes once around in the direction North, East, South and West, keeping the altar to the right. On reaching his position he will use the chisel and mallet upon the rough stone or Ashlar, and then pass the chisel slightly over the smooth or perfect Ashlar.

1st Surv.—Ven.·. M.·..·the first voyage is accomplished.

Ven. M.—We will resume the history of Man's progression in knowledge, at the point where we closed in the First Degree.

The wonderful structure of the human body combines every element of physical knowledge, and man's first lessons in the sciences were combined and wonderfully divided from an examination of his organization, unquestionably the perfection of infinite wisdom. In the right hand, when clenched, he saw a powerful instrument for persuasion, the Mallet furnished him by his Creator,—and his left hand, he saw designed for the skillful management, arrangement and adjustment of the object submitted to the action of the right, and here he has the Chisel. Hence, the mallet is a symbol of the strenth of the right hand, and the chisel of the skill of the left. The human intellect had now made its first step in progressive knowledge, in tracing cause and effect. Man saw that his hands were not acted upon by involuntary muscles—that they were the instruments of a mighty power within him. Hence, the adoption of the mallet as a proper symbol of will, and the chisel of discretion.

Man now discovered that there was a principle within him which placed him superior to all animated creation, and that all was created subject to him and for his use; he had an intuitive knowledge that this principle closely allied him to an infinite creation. To an extent he had the power of creating; he could give new and varied forms, could invent and could imitate, and his hands could give semblance to his ideas. No other created being possessed this power. As the hands were the instruments of this infinite principle, the Mallet has been selected also as a Symbol of the Infinite, and the Chisel of Variety.

Knowledge and instruction having been retained and communicated by the Ancients in symbolic language, we can only attain to a correct translation, and to a literal reading, by reverting to the circumstances surrounding man at that period, and we are surprised on discovering that those opinions which seem to be the result of an elaborate study of man, and to belong to a far advanced philosophy, must have been coeval with man's earliest instructions from the great book of nature. At that period the progress of mind was free, and could pursue its onward course unobstructed; in the progress of ages, formidable obstacles have arisen, and mind has to contend with error and prejudice in its search for light, and is now strengthened, and pleased to trace truth back through the obscurity which has surrounded it, to the period when man's readings of nature were illuminated by the pure light from above.

Ven. M.—Bro.·. Expert, you will proceed on the second voyage with our Bro.·. App.·.

The Ruler in his left hand, the Compasses in his right hand. Travels in the same direction as in the first voyage, keeping the altar at right hand, and at conclusion of the voyage will lay down his implements and imitate the tracing upon the Trestle Board of a horizontal and vertical line, by placing the left hand flat upon the board, fingers vertical and thumb horizontal; and then describe a circle with the vertex of the angle as a centre, by placing the thumb of the right hand at the vertex and with the index finger describe a circumference about the angle.

1st Surv.—Ven.·. M.·., the second voyage is accomplished.

Ven. M.—The mechanical organization of the hand evidently furnished man with his first ideas of the pependicular, and the right angle and the right line, a very valuable and suggestive thought in the initiatory stage of science, as forming the first step to man's progress in all knowledge, to the infinite in wisdom and knowledge; hence, the line and perpendicular may be considered the initial point or unit of all science or knowledge, the beauty and perfection of every mechanical structure depends primarily upon the accuracy of its lines and perpendiculars. The line conveys the ideas of unlimited extent, leading to the Infinite. The compasses on the contrary convey the idea of limited extent, or of the Finite; and the circumference in connection with the right line leads to ideas which connect the Infinite with the Finite, furnishing thought and incentive to mechanical industry·

The Compasses are indicative of the boundaries set to human powers, encompassing the finite with the infinite, showing man that the extent of his powers in comparison with the All-Powerful, is but as a drop to the waters of the vast deep, with the satisfying assurance that the limits to his powers will be enlarged, at each step in his progress, constantly developing objects and truths of manifold variety and interest, leading him step by step to a clearer and more intimate knowledge and perception of the laws governing the Universe, and the attributes of a Divine Intelligence. The restraining influence which preserves the relationship of each point in the circumference to the centre, is the clear perception of truth from error, restraining man within the bounds of reason and sense, preserving him from those visionary flights after a knowledge which may be above that which is written.

VEN. M.—Bro·. Expert, you will proceed on the third voyage.

The Ruler in his left hand, the Lever in his right hand.

Travels in the same direction, and at the conclusion of the voyage, lays down his implements, and with his right hand lifts a small stone, and then uses the Lever in moving a large one.

1st SURV.—Ven.·. M.·., the third voyage is accomplished.

VEN. M.—Man found the perfect Lever represented in his fore arm and elbow, and as the necessity arose for moving masses, his inventive powers were only exercised to bring an application to the assistance of his powers; hence, arose the several varieties of that most valuable of the elementary mechanical principles, the Lever. The intelligence required in adjusting the fulcrum and arms of the Lever, so as to produce the maximum effect, renders the Lever an exceedingly appropriate symbol of weakness made strenth by intellect, or of the power of mind over matter.

You have also the Ruler in company with the Lever, by

7

way of indicating the necessity of subjecting physical force to the operations and control of mind, as well in the exercise of bodily strength as in the adaptation of the mechanical powers to the production of the perfect machine.

Great power comes to naught, or is only productive of evil, unless guided and governed by superior wisdom. Man finds himself surrounded by animal powers of various degrees, all subject to his will, many possessing a physical force far superior to his own, demanding at his hands the exercise of judgment and of mercy. So, in the relations of man to man, where no subjection is ordained, we owe a respectful consideration to the right of the lowly, as to the most exalted. The history of the institution of Freemasonry furnishes many notable instances, and has generally been remarkable for the result of his teachings in this regard.

Deference to the rights of others has ever been her happiest theme, repelling upon all proper occasions the brutal principle, that *right* obtains from *might.*

Bro.·. Expert, please accompany our App.·. on his fourth voyage.

The Square in his right, and the Ruler in his left hand.

Travels in the same direction, and on his return the Apprentice will lay his right hand flat upon the Trestle board, so that his thumb and index finger may form a right angle.

1st Surv.—Ven.·. M.·., the fourth voyage is accomplished.

Ven. M.—In man's first mechanical efforts he was furnished with the " Square" or right angle, by extending the thumb and fore or index finger. In the progress of his structures he found this angle to be of first importance to the stability, beauty, and regularity of his works, and that beauty and stability were the invariable attendants upon regularity. Hence, the square became his most indispensable instrument, and with the ruler in his left hand and the square in his right, he had regularity as the primary distinguishing characteristics of intelligence plainly symbolized.

The Universe with its myriads of worlds and harmony of motion, the wonderful organization of the vegetable and animal creation, even to the most insignificant of the species, gave unmistakable evidence that order and regularity were essential and evident characteristics of Infinite Intelligence. Man found a comfortable assurance of his relationship to the Grand Architect of the Universe, in that, Order was an elemental principle of Intelligence and of Beauty with him as with his Creator.

As we progress in the knowledge of man, of his physical and mental organization, the more clearly do we perceive the close alliance between him and the all wise, and come to view him as a living, breathing, tangible representative of that universal force from which issue life, motion, and all created things.

Bro.·. Expert, you will proceed with our brother upon his fifth and last voyage.

Without implements he travels in the same direction and resumes his position in silence.

· 1st Surv,—Ven.·. M.·., the fifth voyage has been properly performed.

Ven, M.—In this voyage, we have man divested of all implements, and he is here more particularly called to an examination of himself and of the functions pertaining to his physical and mental organization. Man soon discovered that progress and constant change was indelibly stamped upon all things surrounding him, and that progress to maturity and to decay were governed by invariable and immutable laws. In the vegetable world he saw the higher perfections of maturity attained only by cultivation, and that the fertile earth gave forth of the abundance of her increase, save when called for by the labor of man; also in the animals given for man's domestication and use, his cultivation and care was necessary to the development of their highest benefits. Without work the wealth of the earth lay dormant at his feet, and the animal and vegetable productions retroceded to their imperfect, unfruitful condition. So with man, change marks the every moment of his existence; there is no resting point for him until he lays himself down for the last great change, and it is only by constant work and cultivation of his mental and physical faculties that he can reach the perfection of maturity and make the decline of his life, like the descending sun, more and more resplendent to its passing away. As the plant, in the absence of cultivation and of work, man rapidly relapses into a state of barbarism, approaching nearer and nearer to the wild beasts of the forest.

The responsibilities and obligations of man's free agency devolved upon him as soon as he discovered these laws; he saw the road plain before him and the consequences of a departure from it. Hence, man found an abundant and fruitful study in the great and ever present book of nature pointing with unerring finger to the duties he owed to himself.

In truth, such is the object and purport of all the instruction conveyed in this degree, directing man to a correct and intelligent reading from nature of the laws appertaing to his welfare.

You may remember that at your first step into this

symbolic world your attention was called to several interrogatories ;—1st. What does man owe to his fellow-beings? The tenor of the lessons in the first degree. 2d. What does man owe to himself?—and here we have the subject of the second degree. There were others. They are indicative of man's progress in knowledge, of his duties as a man, and of the instruction and train of ideas appertaining to each degree as established in the earlier and purer days of the institution, ere the sacriligious hands of bad men had perverted it to selfish, religious and political ends.

As you progress in your Masonic readings, you will observe that in the Rite which comes to us from England, commonly called the York or English Rite, the lectures and teachings in the Fellow Craft degree is a compendium or dictionary of scientific terms, giving brief and not very intelligible definitions of the Mosaic records of the creation, of the use of artificial globes, of the orders of Architecture, of the human senses, of Grammar, Rhetoric, Logic, Arithmetic, Geometry, Music and Astronomy, embracing the discoveries made in the branches named to the present day. In Scotch Freemasonry we deem these scientific investigations as foreign to the subject matter of the 2d Degree, and a wide departure from Ancient usages.

Science, as it now stands in its various departments, is the result of progress in civilization, was unknown to the Ancients and can not, therefore, be properly embraced in what is called Ancient Craft Masonry. The progress of civilization, the arts and sciences pertain to quite a different order of ideas and form the subject matter of more recent and higher degrees in the Scotch Rite, where full and minute investigations are properly instituted regarding the bearings of recent improvements and discoveries upon the welfare and advancement of man in his progress after a knowledge of the good, the beautiful and the true.

In the Fellow Craft or second degree we conform with the utmost of strictness to the ideas properly appertaining to it, and scrupulously follow the work as observed in the Ancient Institution. We deem it more strictly Masonic as being ground upon which men, of every nation and creed, can stand in the union and fellowship of a happy Fraternity.

Man is here called to an examination of himself that he may attain to a proper estimate of his own position and progress; is shown what he is by the will and dispensation of his Maker, giving him a correct and rational view of himself, of his rights, and of his duties so that he may be the better prepared to withstand the temptations to deviate from the path which leads to honor, to happiness, and to truth as traced for him by his All Wise and Beneficent Father.

The Bro.·. Expert will conduct our brother to the East for our further instruction.

The Expert will let the candidate ascend the steps to the East and stand by the balustrade near to the Secretary.

VEN. M.—We have seen that the exterior world is as a great book, giving us intelligible and truthful readings of nature's laws, leading us to look through nature up to nature's God. Look about you.

The Lodge is a symbol of the world, extending from East to West, from North to South, from the depths of the earth to the celestial heavens. In the East, the rising Sun, the great source of light and heat, shines in the Lodge as the unwearied ruler and guide of our working hours, the symbol of his Creator's power and watchful care, while the Moon, the resplendent orb of night with her attendant stars, reflects the greater glories of divine munificence, diffusing light and harmony in our pathway to Truth, Liberty and Fraternity. .

The Union Cord with Love Knots, which runs around the Lodge upon the Architrave, is indicative of the mystic tie which unites us as brethren in the bonds of a happy Fraternity, telling of full generous love to fellow-men.

The Mosaic Pavement, bordered by the indented tessel is the emblem of the thousand events and accidents with which the frame of our time on earth is filled and as it were chequered, while the richly adorned tesselated border represents the many blessings which surround us. In its center we have the "Blazing Star" within the equilateral triangle. The infinite intelligence overlooking the chequered and variegated scenes of human life. The Finite as coming from and existing in the Infinite.

The Plumb and Level are constant, giving no shadows of deviation, subject to no deflection by extraneous causes. Hence the Plumb has ever been deemed a proper representation of the man who by an undeviating observance of the precepts of equity, is "in conscious virtue bold" and can stand undaunted, erect, before God and man.

The Level is an emblem of Equality, telling us of rights and duties, of pleasures and pains, appertaining alike to all of woman born.

The Trowel, as an instrument, evidently had its origin in the use which man made of the palm of his hand in smoothing the surface of his work in soft materials and has been adopted as an emblem of forgiveness, teaching us so to overlook the asperities, defects, and short comings of our brethren, that we may dwell together in unity. A patient forbearance of what appear to us as weakness in our brother, is essential to harmony in our mystic brotherhood.

You entered with the Twenty-four Inch Guage, a working tool of the App.·. Mas.·., with which you are familiar.

The Rough Ashlar, an unwrought stone, is emblematic of man in his uncultivate 1 state; and the Perfect Ashlar, or wrought stone, is emblematic of man in his more perfect state, when his mind and his passions have been cultivated and subdued by education.

The Three Lights around the altar indicate the points which naturally passed from work to rest, morning, midday and evening, following the march of the Grand Luminary which guides us during our daily labor.

The Trestle or Tracing board, is the emblem of reflection. The wise man will have his plans carefully designed before engaging in any important work. As every feature in the exterior world conveys its lessons of truth, so in this symbolic world—the Lodge—words of wisdom are associated with each and every object, however simple, taking us back to that purer source of light, the fountain of all wisdom, the wondrous works of the Grand Architect of the Universe.

You will now take the obligations required of a Fellow Craft.

Are you ready?

CANDIDATE.—Yes.

VEN. M.—Bro ·. M.·. C.·., you will please take the candidate in charge, and conduct him to the altar.

The candidate will place his right hand upon the square and compasses. The Ven.·. M.·. comes then with a sword in his left hand and a gavel in his right, when the candidate will repeat the following obligation as dictated by the Ven.ˑ. M.ˑ.

OBLIGATION.—" In presence of the Grand Architect of the Universe, under the authority of the Supreme Council of the 33d Degree of the Ancient and Accepted Scotch Rite of Freemasonry, in and for the Sovereign and Independent State of Louisiana, and in presence of this assemblage of Freemasons, I, (*name in full*,) on my word, of honor, do solemnly promise faithfully to keep the *secrets* and *words* of the Fellow Craft Degree, as prescribed by the statutes of the Order ; and I would rather have my heart torn out and thrown to the beasts of prey, than to violate this my solemn promise. So help me God. "

VEN. M.—Truth and the blessings of God be with you.

INVESTITURE OF THIS DEGREE.

The Ven.ˑ. M.ˑ. extends the point of his sword over the candidate's head and says :

"In the name of the Grand Architect of the Universe, under the authority of the Supreme Council of the 33d Degree of the Ancient and Accepted Scotch Rite of Free-Masonry, in and for the Sovereign and Independent State of Louisiana, and by virtue of powers on me conferred, I do hereby make and constitute you a Fellow Craft Mason, of the Ancient and Accepted Scotch Rite, and declare you an active member of the R.ˑ. L.ˑ. (*name and number*.)

Then the Ven.ˑ. M.ˑ. gives five raps with his gavel upon the blade of his sword, goes to the candidate, let the flap of his apron down, shakes hands with him, and resumes his seat in the East.

VEN. M.—Bro.˙. M.˙. C.˙., will please conduct our worthy initiated Brother to the East for our Secret Instructions.

The M.˙. C.˙. will give him a seat near the Sec.˙., where the Ven.˙. M.˙. will approach near to him, and say :

VEN. M.—Admission to a Lodge in this Degree is obtained by rapping at the door, thus. The Ins.˙. Sent.˙. will then open the wicket and ask the password, which you will give in this manner : (*gives him the password.*)

When the door opens for you, you will advance towards the altar, making these steps, (*shows him,*) and then give the sign of Fellow Craft (*thus*) to the Ven.˙. M.˙. in the East, then face about to the left, give the same sign to the 1st Surv.˙., sitting in the West, then facing to the right, giving the same sign to the 2d Surv.˙. in the South. Then take a seat under the column " J "—that letter is the initial of the sacred word in this Degree, and is given thus, (*gives him the word.*) The word and grip must always be given together, thus.

The Battery is given, (*thus.*)

The Ven.˙. M.˙. then resumes his seat.

VEN. M.—M.˙. C.˙., you will conduct our Bro.˙. (*name,*) to the 1st Surv.˙. for examination in our secret instructions.

At the conclusion the 1st Surv.˙. says :

1st SURV.—(*raps*)Ven.˙. M.˙., his instructions are correct.

VEN. M.—Bro.˙. M.˙. C.˙., please give Bro.˙. (*name,*) a seat upon the East for this day.

The M.˙. C.˙. will give him a seat near the Sec.˙.

VEN. M.—Bro.˙. M.˙. C.˙., please proclaim, from the East, that Bro.˙. (*name,*) has been duly and legally constituted a

Fellow Craft Mason, in the Ancient and Accepted Scotch Rite; that he has given the solemn obligation, and received secret instructions of the Degree, and invite the fraternity to receive and protect him accordingly.

PROCLAMATION.

MAST. C.—Be it known from East to West, from North to South, that Bro.·. (*name,*) has been legally passed to the Fellow Craft Degree in the Ancient and Accepted Scotch Rite, and admitted as an active member of the R.·. L.·. (*name and number,*) in the East of .... under the authority of the Supreme Council of Ins.·. Gen.·. of the 33d Degree, in and for the Sovereign and Independent State of Louisiana, and the Fraternity are invited to receive and protect him accordingly.

The concluding ceremonies of this Degree are the same as in the App.·. Degree, observing the proper Sign and Battery.

The Orator is then called upon for a lecture upon the Degree.

The Visiting Brothers will receive the usual compliments in the 2d Degree.

The Lodge must be formally closed in the 2d Degree, when work can be resumed in the 1st Degree.

At its conclusion the Lodge must be formally closed in the 1st Degree, and the workmen called off for refreshment, "remembering before they part to renew their solemn obligations of secrecy."

LECTURE ON THE SECOND DEGREE.

Ven. M.—Bro.·. 1st Surv.·., are you a Fellow Craft Mason?

1st Surv.—Ven.·. M.·., I am, try me,

Q.—Why did you receive the Degree of Fellow Craft?

A.—In order to work to the best of my strength and ability with all Freemasons, my companions and brethren, to the final triumph of Masonic principles.

Q.—What is the great work contemplated by Freemasons?

A.—To make all men equal by labor; and a perfect equality will never reign in this world unless the principles of true Freemasonry are known and put in practice.

Q.—How were you received a Fellow Craft?

A.—My eyes wide open, and in the plenitude of my strength and freedom.

Q.—What did you see on entering the Lodge?

A.—Two large columns or pillars, one at the left hand of the 1st Surveillant with the letter " B," and the other at his right hand with the letter " J."

Q.—What was their composition?

A.—Molten or Cast Brass.

Q.—What were their dimensions?

A.—Eighteen cubits in height, twelve in circumference, and four in diameter.

Q.—Why were they cast hollow?

A.—The better to preserve the tools and archives of Freemasonry, and also the money destined to the payment of Fellow Crafts and Apprentices.

Q.—How did you gain admission?

A.—By a sign, by a pass word and a sacred word, and by a grip.

Q.—Give me the sign.

A.—(*The sign is given.*)

Q.—What does it denote?

A.—That I should rather have my heart torn out by the roots than to violate the promise I made in presence of my brethren assembled in this Lodge.

Q.—Give the pass word to Bro.·.———

A.—(*The pass word is given*)

Q.—Give the sacred word to Bro∴——

A.—(*The sacred word is given.*)

Q.—Give the grip to Bro∴——

A.—(*The grip is given.*)

Q.—How were you disposed of after you entered the Lodge?

A.—I made five royages. In the first I had in my hand a Mallet and a Chisel, in the second, a Ruler and a pair of Compasses, in the third, a Ruler and a Lever, in the fourth, a Ruler and a Square.

Q.—What is the use of these different tools?

A·—The Mallet and Chisel serve to pare and hew the rough stone, in taking off its asperity and giving it its proper form.

The Ruler and Compasses are tools by which lines are drawn on plain and smooth surfaces.

The Lever is destined to raise heavy bodies, and the Square to form equal sides and right angles.

Q.—What is the moral and symbolical meaning of these tools

A.—By the Mallet and Chisel, we mean that a true Freemason ought to divest himself of his prejudices and vices. By the Ruler, that our actions ought to be governed and measured by the eternal principles of morality. By the Compasses, that we ought to contain ourselves in the limits of truth and justice. By the Lever, that it is our duty to oppose a determined resistance to all that is arbitrary and despotic; and by the` Square, that we ought to square our actions by the opinions of good men, and our lives by the precepts of philosophers.

Q.—How did you make the fifth voyage?

A.—With my hands entirely free.

Q.—Why?

A.—As an indication to the Fellow Craft, that it is only, after a long and tedious labor, that he will be permitted to rest and enjoy in his freedom and independence.

Q.—Has our Lodge any ornaments?

A.—It has. 1st. The Mosaic or chequered pavement, representing this world, which, though chequered over with good and evil, yet brethren may work together thereon and not stumble;—2d. The Blazing Star as a symbol of the true light which Freemasonry spreads over the whole world;—And 3d. The Cord of Union which surrounds our Lodge, teaching all Freemasons to live together as a family of brethren, in order to better defend all their political, religious, civil and social rights

Q.—Has your Lodge any jewels ?

A.—It has; six, three moveable and three immoveable.

Q.—What are the three moveable jewels ?

A.—The Level, Plumb and Trowel.

Q.—What do they teach?

A.—The Level equality; the Plumb, rectitude of life and conduct, and the Trowel, teaching all Freemasons that they ought not only to forgive their mutual wrongs and offences, but also to cement and strengthen the ties of brotherhood.

Q.—What are the three immoveable jewels?

A—The Rough Ashlar, the Perfect Ashlar and the Trestle Board.

Q.—What do they represent?

A.—The Rough Ashlar represents man in his rude and imperfect state of nature; the Perfect Ashlar represents man in that state of perfection to which we all hope to arrive by means of a virtuous life and education; and the Trestle Board is the emblem of reflection and wisdom.

Q.—Where do the Fellow Crafts sit in the Temple ?

A.—In the South or in the North.

Q,—Why in the South?

A.—To help Master Masons in their works, and to profit by their lessons.

Q.—Why in the North?

A.—To assist the Apprentices in their works.

Q —How do the Fellow Crafts work.

A.—With Joy, Fervor and Freedom.

Q.—What is your age as a Fellow Craft ?

A.—Five years.

THIRD DEGREE.

OFFICERS,

A Most Respectable Master.
A Most Venerable 1st Surveillant.
A Most Venerable 2d Surveillant.
A Most Venerable Orator.
A Most Venerable Secretary.
A Most Venerable Expert.
A Most Venerable Treasurer
A Most Venerable Master of Ceremonies.
A Most Venerable Inside Sentinel.

All Brethren are designed under the appellation of Venerable Brethren.

PREPARATION OF THE LODGE FOR INITIATION,

The Lodge must be hung in black, strewed with tears or symbols of death. The table and altar covered with black palls. The arrangements for lighting the Lodge, when desired, must be abundant either with gas or candles. During the ceremonies, no lights are permitted save those hereafter designated. The altar shall be furnished with the square and compasses placed masonically. The three tripods surrounding the altar must be supplied with unlighted candles.

THE EAST.—On the table of the R∴. M∴. there will be placed a Maul, the head of which must be stuffed with wool or cotton, and covered with black cloth or leather.

A transparent, dimly lighted, surmounted by a skull with this device plainly written across the transparency, " In the midst of life we are in death."

Near to and in front of the Master's table there will be placed a large transparency, representing a chequered or Mosaic pavement, upon which is a coffin covered with a black pall strewed with tears and sculls. There will also be represented upon it a tree, so designed that " the cross" shall be apparent, with a branch of "Acacia," with three limbs, one extending upon each horizontal arm of the cross and one upon the upper vertical arm.

On the upper vertical arm will also be placed a "Blazing Star," within an equilateral triangle and at the foot of the cross will be placed the square and compasses forming a lozenge.

PREPARATION IN THE WEST.—On the table will be a transparency dimly lighted with this inscription, "Life comes out of death." Upon the transparency will be a human skull. Upon the table there will be a roll of paper nine inches in circumference and eighteen inches in length, also a pair of large compasses made of wood having iron points.

PREPARATION IN THE SOUTH —On the table, a transparency with this inscription, "*Do thy work and die without fear.*"

A roll of paper as in the West, also a flat Ruler, twenty four inches.

PREPARATION OF CANDIDATE,

The M∴. E,∴. assumes charge of the candidate in an

adjoining room, divests him of coat, waistcoat, cravat and shoes, receives his watch, money, knife, keys and all metallic substances he may have about him; his left arm and shoulder must be withdrawn from the sleeve of his shirt and undershirt, so as to be entirely naked, and a small silver square will be tied upon his naked arm, just above the elbow, with a black ribbon. A cord will be girded around his loins three times. He will wear his apron as a Fellow Craft.

OPENING OF THE LODGE.

The Lodge must be formally opened in the 1st, 2d and 3d Degrees, successively, following the general directions given in the Ritual of the 1st Degree, giving the Sign and Battery pertaining to each Degree,---great care being observed that all present are entitled to seats.

RECEPTION OF VISITORS.

The M∴ C∴ will visit the anti-chamber and avenues, and bring the visitors' register to the M∴ R∴ M∴, who will give directions regarding the reception of visitors.

Announcement of the object of the meeting by the M∴ R∴ M∴ calling for objections to the initiation, giving them due consideration, and if there are none, he will ask for a unanimous assent on the part of all present. same as in the 1st Degree.

9

INITIATION.

The M∴ C∴ causes the candidate to rap at the door as a Fellow Craft.

The Inside Sentinel looks through the wicket, and reports to the 1st Surv∴.

1st Surv. —M∴ R∴ M,∴, there is a Fellow Craft raping at the door.

M. R M.—Bro.∴ Expert, ascertain who is thus rudely disturbing our meditations.

The Expert goes to the anti-chamber, makes the proper inquiries, returns, leaving the door slightly ajar, and from it reports.

Expert.—M∴ R∴ M∴, one of our Brothers is at the door having in charge a Fellow Craft.

M. R. M.—Bro.∴ Conductor, how does that Fellow Craft expect to gain admission to our presence and to our solemnities?

M∴ C∴,—By virtue of the word of pass.

M. R. M.—Through the word of pass? That is exceedingly strange, and sufficient cause for the most fearful apprehensions!—for, how could he have obtained possession of that word save than by a participation in the horrid crime which we fear has been committed. See that no stain of blood besmears his hands or clothing, and bring us his apron.

Expert.—M∴ R∴ M∴, we have carefully examined that Fellow Craft and find him clear from suspicion of having participated in that most foul and abhorrent deed; his hands are clean, and his apron, which I bring you, is spotless.

The Expert takes the apron to the East, and resumes his seat.

M. R. M.—Bro∴ 1st Surv∴, will you go and examine the Fellow Craft, search carefully for any trace, mark or spot, by which we may learn of the fate of our most M∴ R. . M∴.

1st Surv.—(*after complying, says:*—M∴ R∴ M∴, a strict examination fails to elicit anything which can justly attach suspicion to that Fellow Craft. ·

M. R. M.—It being so, go out again and ask him for the word of pass.

The 1st Surv∴ goes out and says to the candidate.

1st Surv.—Give me the word of pass.

Candidate.—(*Says,*)I cannot, my conductor will give it for me.

The 1st Surv∴ then asks and receives it from the M∴ C∴ in a whisper.

1st Surv.—M∴ R∴ M∴ that Fellow Craft could not give me the word of pass; he relied upon his conductor, who gave it correctly.

M. R. M.—Let him enter.

The M∴ C∴ takes the ends of the cord which girds the candidate, and makes him enter backwards as far as the altar, where he will stand with his face to the door or West.

M. R. M.—Bro∴ Fellow Craft, you find us surrounded with the solemn paraphernalia of Death, engaged in contemplating the momentous mysteries attendant upon man's final laying down to rest in the arms of the dread conqueror. Man is subject to that unalterable decree of the Almighty, "Of dust thou art, and unto dust shalt thou return;" and "the spirit shall return unto God who gave it." Death, when the result of natural causes, may be met with a cheerful, happy reliance, comforting to those whose hearth stones have been made desolate at the hands of the fell destroyer; but our hearts are appalled when our dear friends are suddenly sent, by the inhumanity of man, to their last final resting place, to stand unannounced before their Maker.

You find us thus cast down with the most hopeless of sorrows, at the fearful apprehension of a most unnatural death to our most Resp∴. Master. No trace of him has yet been discovered. A recent corpse has been found and brought in, which you will see in the coffin at your left, but it is not that of our Master. Its shocking mutilation has added greatly to our fears and anxiety regarding his fate. As he possessed knowledge, and held a secret of vast import to the advancement of the Fellow Craft, we fear he has fallen a victim to the overreaching reckless ambition of wicked and unprincipled men of that Degree ; and that in him truth and integrity has been crushed to earth by the violent hands of intrigue and oppression. Bro∴. Fellow Craft, have you any knowledge of a conspiracy against his life, or have you in any way or manner participated in his overthrow?

CANDIDATE.—No.

M. R. M.—Then turn your face to the East, and tell us if you will patiently and earnestly give us your assistance in our search for the fallen.

CANDIDATE.—Yes.

M. R. M.—Now it will be impossible for you to join us in this most worthy pursuit until admitted to a full participation in the secrets and mysteries of the Master's Degree.

Are you prepared to undergo the fearful trials, incident to this most instructive initiation ?

CANDIDATE.—Yes.

M. R. M.—Bro∴. Conductor, you may proceed with your charge upon the first voyage.

Travels from North to East, keeping the altar at the right

hand, giving the App.·. sign, as he passes the East, South and West, and as each Officer answers the sign he will give three raps. Brings the candidate to the altar. from thence takes him to the 2d Surv.·., when the candidate will give the App.·. rap upon the table. The 2d Surv.·. rises, places his roll of paper on the nape of the neck of the candidate as to detain him, and says:

2d Surv.—Who comes here?

· M. C.—A Fellow Craft who has served his full time, and desires to be raised to the Master's Degree.

2d Surv.—How does he expect to gain admission ?

M. C.—Through the word of pass.

2d Surv.—How is it possible for him to give it?

M. C.—I, his conductor, will give it for him.

2d Surv.—Give it to me.

M. C.—(*In a whisper.*) T.·.

2d Surv.— Let him pass.

The M.·. C.·. Leads the candidate to the altar.

2d Surv..—Bro.·. 1st Surv.·., the candidate has passed the South correctly.

1st Surv—(*Raps.*) M.·. R.·. M.·., the 2d voyage has been correctly performed.

M. R. M —Bro.·. conductor, you may proceed with the candidate upon his second voyage.

The second voyage is performed as the first, giving the Fellow Craft's sign, and when the candidate has reached his place at the altar he will proceed to the West and give the rap of the Fellow craft upon that officer's table.

The 1st Surv.·. will rise, place his roll of paper upon the candidate's breast and say :

1st Surv.—Who comes here? Further questions and answers are given as at the South, and when the candidate has resumed his place by the altar:—

1st Surv.—(*Raps.*) M.·. R.·. M.·., the candidate has passed the West and completed his second voyage correctly.

M. R. M.—Bro.·. conductor, please proceed upon the third voyage.

Travels in the same direction. No signs or raps are given, and the candidate quietly resumes his position by the altar.

1st Surv —(*Raps.*) M.·. R.·.M.·., the third voyage is accomplished·

M. R. M.—These three voyages, my Bro.·., recall the last sad scene of all, the final panorama of youth, manhood and senility· At the conclusion of man's tumultuous voyage of life, his every action passes in quick review before him and the various scenes of his life come up to his mind as with the speed of thought· All the sins of his life will dart their venemous fangs into his very soul, calling for judgment at his own hands.

Happy the man who can lay down to his final rest with a conscience void of offence towards God and man, and as he is parting from earth can view the fading scenes of his life, with a forgiving and a repentant heart· Then is death robbed of his sting and the grave of its victory. The good man goes down to his grave with the blessings of the living and death lays him upon a bed of glory, for he will hear the joyful acclamation of "Well done, Thou good and faithful servant."

You will now take the Master Mason's obligation.

The M.·. C.·. will cause the candidate to place his hands, his right hand over the left, resting upon the square and compasses· All present rise as witnesses.

The M.·. R.·. M.·. goes to the altar and causes the candidate to repeat from his dictation,

OBLIGATION.—" In presence of the G∴ A∴ O∴ T∴ U∴, under the authority of the Supreme Council of the 33d Degree of the Ancient and Accepted Scotch Rite of Freemasonry, in and for the Sovereign and Independent State of Louisiana, with this assemblage of Master Masons as witnesses, I (name in full,) upon my sacred word of honor, do hereby solemnly promise never to reveal the secrets, words and mysteries of the Master Mason's Degree, never to speak thereon except to a regular Master of the same Rite, or in a regular and legally constituted Lodge thereof, and I do, furthermore, give my sacred promise to do no unjustifiable violence or in any manner to defame or otherwise harm a brother Mason, his mother, sister, wife or daughter, but to be to them as a true and faithful brother and to assist them in their adversity to the extent of my ability. Also to obey the general statutes of the Scotch Rite, the regulations of the Supreme Council for the State of Louisiana, the by-laws of this Lodge, and cause the same to be obeyed.

I would rather have my body severed into two parts, my bowels torn out and burned, and the ashes thereof scattered to the winds, than to violate this my solemn obligation—So help me God."

M. R. M.—God grant that you may never be prompted to violate so sacred an obligation!

The M∴ R∴ M∴ then removes the cord from the candidate's loins, puts upon him the Fellow Craft's apron, leaves him behind the altar, resumes his seat in the East, requests all to be seated, the M∴ C∴ giving the candidate a seat.

M. R. M.—The instruction conveyed in this degree is as important as the ceremonies are impressive. Constituting as it does the last of the purely symbolic degrees, it is important that its teachings should be clearly comprehended; and that you may acquire strength to withstand its trials and a proper state of mind to duly receive its instruction, we will relate something of its history and of the terrible legend connected therewith.

The degree is founded upon and draws its lesson from a legendary account of circumstances and events which transpired at the building of Solomon's temple at Jerusalem.

From the Bible, we learn that at the time when Saul ascended the throne of Judah, the people of that country were quite ignorant of the mechanic arts. There was not a man among them who could work in iron. They were obliged to call upon their most bitter enemies, the Philistines, to have even their instruments of husbandry sharpened and repaired. Their swords and halberds were not of their own making. David saw the necessity of cultivating in them a taste for the mechanic arts, and sent for all the foreigners in his dominions, that he might select from among them, builders, hewers, stone-cutters, carpenters and all manner of cunning men for every manner of work. Notwithstanding, David had commanded all the Princes of Israel to help Salomon, he was obliged to ask Hiram, King of Tyre, for help, saying "for thou knowest that there is not among us any that can skill to hew timber like unto the Sidonians." So Hiram, the King, sent him a skillful carpenter and stone-cutter, Adoniram, to superintend the workmen in wood and stone at mount Lebanon.

"And King Salomon sent and fetched Hiram out of Tyre. He was a widow's son of the tribe of Naphtali, and his father was a man of Tyre, a worker in brass; and he was filled with wisdom and understanding, and cunning to work all works in brass. And he came to King Solomon and wrought all his work."

Hiram cast two pillars of brass of wondrous work and curious device, a particular description of which is given in (1 King, chap. 7; v. 15-20.)

"And he set up the pillars in the porch of the temple; and he set up the right pillar and called the name thereof, *Jachin;* and he set up the left pillar and called the name thereof,—*Boaz,* v, 21."

In 2 Chron., chapter 2d, v. 13 and 14, the King of Tyre writes to Solomon thus, "And now I have sent a cunning man, indued with understanding. He is the son of woman of the daughter of Dan, and his father was a man of Tyre, skillful to work in gold and in silver, in brass, in iron, in stone and in timber, in purple, in blue, in fine linen, and in crimson; also to grave any manner of graving, and to find out any device which shall be put to him with thy cunning menand with the cunning men of my Lord David, thy father."

We also read v. 17 and 18, "And Solomon numbered all the strangers that were in Israel, and they were found an hundred and fifty thousand, and three thousand and six hundred, (153,600.) and he set three score and ten thousand of them to be bearers of burdens, (70,000.), and four score thousand to be hewers in the mountain, (80,000.), and three thousand six hundred, (3,600.) overseers to let the people work."

We learn from a legend or tradition of equal antiquity, that Solomon in his wisdom so arranged and classified this great body of men, that neither envy, discord nor confusion were suffered to interrupt or disturb the peace and good fellowship which prevailed among the workmen. They were divided into three classes : Apprentices, Fellow Crafts and Masters. A certain number of each class composed a company or Lodge, in charge of an able master. Over all was Hiram, the widow's son, filled with wisdom and understanding.

The more readily to insure order among so large a body of strangers, of various degrees of skill, King Solomon with the King of Tyre and the learned architect Hiram, adopted certain signs, grips and words, so as easily and correctly to distinguish the several orders and classes of workmen.

Now it was the custom of their Grand Master Hiram, to enter the Temple, at high twelve, each day, while the workmen were at rest, and offer up his devotions to the Almighty Maker and Father of the Universe.

Here the M. R. M. gives a tap and the brethren rise. The M. C. leads the candidate to the altar.

M. R. M.—He approached the altar and humbly upon his knees said :

"Almighty Maker and Father of the Universe, Thou art the only true and everliving God and Creator of all that exists, enlighten my mind with true knowledge and wisdom; let charity, love to fellow-men, and to Thee, prevail in my heart; and give me strength of body and of mind so to perform the work Thou hast appointed, in accordance with Thy will. Grant that the workmen upon this Thy house may humbly look to Thee for guidance in the ways of virtue and of knowledge, and that they may see and understand that the heart of man is the only true and acceptable temple for the worship and glory of Thee. Amen, amen, amen."

When he had so prayed, he rose and took his way towards the door at the South.

The M∴ C∴ leads the candidate to the South, and the

2d Surv∴ seizes him by the throat with his left hand, holding the Rule in his right, when the M∴ R∴ M∴, says:

M. R. M.—But there he met with a Fellow Craft, armed with a·ruler, who seized him by the throat and said :

2d Surv.—Give me the Master's grip.

Candidate.—I cannot give it except in presence of Solo· mon and the King of Tyre.

˙2d Surv.—Give me the Master's grip.

Candidate.—I cannot.

2d Surv.—Give me the Master's grip.

Candidate.—I cannot.

The 2d Surv∴ then rudely but lightly strikes the candidate upon the side of the neck with the ruler.

M. R. M.—Being so abused and struck at the South, Hiram staggered back and proceeded to the door at the West.

While this is being said the M∴ C∴ leads the candidate to the West, and the 1st Surv∴ seizes him at the breast with the left hand, holding the open compasses in his right.

M. R. M.—But there again he met another Fellow Craft, armed with the Compasses, who seized him by the breast, and said :   .

1st Surv.—Give me the M∴ M∴ grip and word ?

Candidate.—I cannot give it except in the presence of King Solomon and the King of Tyre·

1st Surv.—Give me the M∴ M∴ grip and word.

Candidate.—I cannot.

1st Surv.—Give me the M∴ M∴ grip and word·

Candidate.—I cannot.

Then the 1st Surv∴ roughly but harmlessly strikes him upon the bare breast with a point of the compasses.

M. R. M.—Weak and fainting from the blow, Hiram endeavored to escape by the door at the East.

While this is being said the M∴ C∴ leads the candidate to the East, and the M∴ R∴ M∴ seizes him by the chest and says:

M. R. M.—Give me the Masters' Sacred Word.

CANDIDATE.—I cannot give it save in the presence of King Solomon, Hiram and the King of Tyre.

M. R· M.—Give it to me?

CANDIDATE.—I cannot.

M. R. M.—Give it to me, I say?

CANDIDATE.—I cannot.

Then the M∴ R∴ M∴ strikes him upon the forehead with his stuffed maul, when two Brothers seize him and lay him in a coffin, which had been concealed from the candidate's sight. A pall is spread over so as not to obstruct his breathing, and the coffin removed to the corner of the Lodge, at the 2d Surv's left hand. The small silver square is removed from his arm and placed upon his breast, and a branch of Acacia is placed to stand at the head, or thrown upon the pall. In the mean time all leave the Lodge, except the officers, and after an apparent consultation they also leave, having a care to shut the door.

In a few seconds the officers return and light the Lodge, to the fullest extent. The M∴ R∴ M∴ goes to his seat.

M. R. M.—(*Rap,*) Bro∴ Exp∴, will you ring the bell that the workmen may be called from refreshment and rest.

The Expert rings the bell, which is placed between West and South· The BB∴ come in, but instead of going to their respective seats, they assemble in small groups at various points and seem anxious to communicate something mysterious to each other, soon the M. R. *M.* says:

M. R. M.—Bro.·. Expert, the laborers have been called to work and the hour is passed, and yet our Grand Master has not appeared. 'Tis exceeding strange, and we fear he has been detained by some serious accident. Will you try and ascertain the cause of his absence?

The Expert leaves the altar, travels from East to South and West, leaves the Lodge for a few seconds, returns to the altar and says :

EXPERT.—M.·. R.·., M.·. after diligent search and inquiry in every direction, I have only been enabled to learn this much :

Our Grand Master was seen to enter the Temple at midday, as was his custom, for devotion, but from that moment all trace of him is lost. As I was cautiously returning, I heard a voice at the South, which said :

2d SURV.—Oh! would to God that my throat had been cut across and my tongue torn out by the roots, ere I had been accessory to the death of so good a man as our Grand Master, Hiram!

EXPERT —Immediately hereafter I heard a voice in the West, which said :

1st SURV.—Oh! would to God that my heart had been torn from my breast and thrown to beasts of prey, ere I had conspired to take the life of so good a man as our Grand Master, Hiram!

EXPERT.—And I heard a lamentable voice from the East, which said:

M.·. R.·. M.·.—Oh! great is my sorrow!—Would to God that my body had been severed into two parts, my bowels torn out and burned, and the ashes scattered to the winds of Heaven, ere I had given the fatal blow to our Grand Master, Hiram!

Immediately eleven Brethern (if not convenient a less number,) with the M.·. C.·. at their head, arrange themselves in a semi-circle about the steps at the East, with their heads cast mournfully down, when the M.·. C.·. says:

M. C.—M.·. R.·. M.·., we can no longer withstand the shame and remorse with which we are oppressed. We have committed a grievous wrong and are heartily sorry. As the Temple is near being finished, we wickedly and foolishly conspired to possess ourselves by force of the Master's secret, sign, words and grip, that we might hereafter enjoy the benefits and privileges of the mastership, without being subjected to the requiremens and trials exacted of candidates. Our better judgment prevailed, and we withdrew from the horrible conspiracy, and do now humbly confess our great wrong. We fear that our Grand *Master* has fallen a victim to our wicked designs at the hands of three Fellow Crafts, who are now strangely absent.

M. R. M.—Who are they ?

M. C.—Jubela, Jubelo and Jubelum.

M. R. M—Our Grand *Master* has undoubtedly been murdered by them. Let justice have its full course with them. As for us we have a solemn duty to perform, in searching for and paying the last sad honors to the remains of our beloved Grand *Master.*

The *M.·. R.·. M.·.* takes a position at the foot of the steps to the East, with his face to the East; the 1st Surv.·. takes position at his left and the 2d Surv.· at his right. The *M.·. C.·.* arranges all the Brethren present in three columns, behind the three officers, with their faces to the East.

M. R. M.—Bro.·. 2d Surv.·., proceed with your column to the North and West and make diligent search.

The 2d Surv.·. leads his column to the left, passing by

the head of the other columns, and when he reaches the coffin, he picks up a sprig of Acacia and says :

2d Surv.—Brothers, the earth has recently been disturbed here, let us examine closely.

He raises a corner of the pall, takes the silver square, measures the coffin from East to West, replaces the square and pall, plants the bough of Acacia by the head, and returns with the column.

2d Surv.—*M.*∴ R... *M.*∙, we have found a mound of fresh earth not far hence, having the appearance of a stealthily made grave, measuring full six feet from East to West, where we planted an Acacia bough as a sign of recognition.

M. R. M.—Bro∴ 1st Surv.∴, hasten with your column and make further observation regarding that mound∙

The 1st Surv.∴ leads his column to the right, goes to the South, to the West, and then to the coffin, and says :

1st Surv.—Here is the Acacia, we will examine.

Raises a corner of the pall, measures from North to South upon the coffin with the silver square; replaces it ; places a sprig of Acacia in the left hand of the candidate ; places his right hand across his breast so that a right angle may be formed at the elbow, and between the thumb and forefinger replaces the pall, and returns with his column by the North, and takes his position at the M.∴ R.∙∙ M's.∴ left hand, and says :

1st Surv.—We found the spot marked by the Acacia, and an excavation six feet from North to South ; exposed a corpse, and presuming it to be that of our Grand Master, Hiram Abif, we placed a branch of Acacia in his left hand as a sign of recognition.

M. R. *M.*—That is undoubtedly the corpse of our Grand Master, let us put on our aprons and endeavor to raise it from its bed of violence.

The three columns start together, march to the right, and proceed from South to West, then to the coffin, marching slowly twice around it. The M∴ R∴ M∴ standing at the foot, takes the sprig of Acacia from the candidate's hands, and says :

M. R. M.—Behold the Acacia! From death comes life eternal! This is a true sign our Grand Master's remains lie smouldering here.

The M∴ R∴ M∴ then removes the pall, and with the silver square measures the depth of the coffin, and exclaims

M. R. M.—Six feet in depth.

He then examines the corpse, stands erect, raises both hands, so as to form a right angle at the elbow, then interlaces the fingers of both hands, palms turned outwards, passing the back of his hands against his forehead and exclaims :

M. R. M.—Oh Lord! Oh Lord! (*keeping the fingers interlaced he will let the hands fall to the navel.*) This is indeed the corpse of our Grand Master. Let us try to lift it out.

The 2d Surv∴, giving the candidate the Apprentice grip, drops the candidate's hand, and says :

2d Surv.—Boaz! the skin cleaves from the bones.

The 1st Surv∴ then gives the Fellow Craft grip, lets his hand drop and says :

1st Surv,—Jachin! The flesh is corrupted and putrified to the bones.

M. R. M.—Hold, Brothers! Do you not see that it is only by united efforts that we can succeed?

The 2d Surv∴ stands at the left, the 1st Surv∴ at the head, the M∴ R∴ M∴ at the right, and says :

M. R. M.—We will try the Master's grip.

Gives him the Master's grip. All seize hold and raise him carefully from the coffin, the M∴ R∴ M.', exclaims :

M.R.M.—M........ ! this is the son of putrifaction

The M∴ R∴ M∴ gives him the five points thus:—places his right foot and knee against the Candidate's right foot and knee, breast to breast, left hands embracing the person over the right shoulder, mouth to ear. The M∴ R∴ M∴ says to the Candidate : "I will now give you the sacred word, it is never to be communicated except in this manner, (gives him the word M∴) These are called the five points of perfection : Hand to hand means that we are bound to serve each other; knee to knee that we profess one common belief, the unity of God; foot to foot that we will walk together as Brethren in the path of truth and justice; hand to back that we will never revile a brother behind his back, but rather support and defend him; breast to breast that we will preserve our secrets inviolate, lest in an unguarded moment we betray the solemn trust confided to our honor.

All resume their seats, the M∴ C∴ giving the candidate a seat behind the altar. The M∴ R∴ M∴ may then give an account of the Egyptian mysteries.

M. R. M.—In the Ancient mysteries of Isis, celebrated by the Egyptians, the candidate to the Third Degree was introduced into a hall; over its door was written : "These are the Gates of Death." Coffins and mummies stood in niches around the walls, and near the entrance a naked recent corpse was lying. In the centre was the tomb of Osiris, presenting many spots of fresh blood, indicative of a violent death. The candidate was asked if he had participated in that murder. The many years which have elapsed since the death of Osiris would render the question absurd, unless asked in the sense of an allegory· The candidate was then conducted to another hall, where he met with the initiated, all clothed in funeral black· A crown was presented to him which he stamped beneath his feet, and all exclaimed, "Vengeance, vengeance, vengeance." The candidate was slightly struck upon the head with a sacrificial ax; he was then seized and bandaged like a mummy, while the spectator exhibited great sorrow and regret· When thus clothed as for the grave, he was arraigned before a dread tribunal, for the murder of Osiris, tried and acquitted. On attaining his liberty, he was instructed in Egyptian Geography and Astronomy. The sign of recognition consisted in an embrace, which symbolized a belief in the res. urrection of the dead and the reproduction of life by death. We thus have a complete sketch of the Egyptian initiation, and you will not fail to observe the close resemblance between it and the one through which you have just passed· Indeed, there can be no question that our ideas of Masonry have come to us from the Egyptians. The legend has been changed to the period of King Solomon· We do not know whether it was done by him or at a more recent period· He may have embodied in the legend circumstances connected with the period of his reign, for the purpose of com. memoration, as did Isis in honor of her slaughtered husband Osiris.

The spirit and intent of the initiation is plainly derived from the ancient Egyptian mysteries, and if it is indebted to Solomon for its traditional historical readings, he certainly could have had but one object in view in rendering it more acceptable to his people by engrafting upon the original and prevailing idea of the mystic art, ceremonies commemorative of events which had proved most gratifying to the national pride of a people who believed themselves the chosen of God.

In considering the more reasonable hypothesis, the adoption at a more recent period of the legend, founded upon incidents recorded in Jewish history, and more particularly concerning the erection of Solomon's Temple at Jeruzalem, as given to us in the sacred writings, for the purpose of allaying the bitter persecutions by which the institution had suffered most severely at the hands of the Papal power which had yielded to the intolerance of a bigotry unsurpassed in malignity.

No other rational suppositions have ever been presented regarding the original adoption of the historical part of the Third Degree, either of which precludes the very idea of its original design for the propagation of any religious creed whatsoever. It is thus that the Ancient and Accepted Scotch Rite finds its peculiar mission to be the preservation, in all its ancient integrity, of a purely philosophical institution, as handed down to us by our forefathers.

The Third Degree is plainly intended to remind us by impressive ceremonies of the great law of our physical being, that we must all pass through the gates of death in our journeying to the higher life, and that all there is of earth in our organization must return to its original elements, supplying nutriment and material for successive generations of vegetable and animal organizations. Thus much for its elucidation of physical law. It also tells of our higher obligations. Love to God and love to fellow-men. In the poor widow's son, born to the lowly condition of a servant and subject, rising to an honorable association with Kings, the wisest and most learned, we have an example fraught with the beauty of simplicity, showing the reward which awaits honest, unpretending industry. When admitted to the confidence of the two most mighty Kings upon earth, Hiram, the personification of Truth, Fidelity and Justice, was waylaid by Falsehood, Deceit and Violence in the form of three assassins, Jubela, Jubelo and Jubelum and although cast down and crushed to earth, Truth rises triumphant by the five points of perfection, and is cherished through time by a brotherhood unsurpassed in all that is honorable and true to manhood. We here see Truth, Fidelity and Justice portrayed as the elements of love to God and love to man, made the chief corner stone in that Temple, not made with hands, eternal in the heavens.

In the ceremonies you were struck upon the neck, heart and head, the parts where the vital forces are most readily reached, teaching us the necessity of exercising constant restraint upon the tongue as the utterer of falsehood, upon the heart as the source of deceit, the parent of falsehood, and upon the head which gives direction and power to those active enemies of Truth.

Your descent into a coffin and rising therefrom, marks the great metamorphosis when all that is mortal of man returns to mother earth, and the immortal soars to realms unknown. So it becomes the Neophyte on being raised to this degree to endeavor to force the crude materials of his nature into subjection and to rise superior to the infirmities of flesh and the world.

The Acacia which hung over your symbolic grave is an emblem coeval with the institution of Freemasonry, and is of unknown antiquity.

Some attribute its adoption as a funeral bough, in signification of the resurrection to Solomon. We read that the disciples of Zoroaster had their mysteries bough; the

Egyptians their Lotus; the Eleusinians their Myrtle, and the Druids their Mistletoe. The Acacia was a well known symbol among the Arabians of fraternity and alliance, and has ever been so considered by the Mahomedans. There is, therefore, little or no question but that the symbol comes to us from the Masons of the desert, the Arabs. We have other conclusive evidence of the signification of the symbol in the circumstance that the "sign of distress," the "call for help" and the sprig of Acacia are made concomitant and appeal to Fraternal Alliance, disconnected from allusion to death on a future state.

Bro∴ M∴ C∴, permit our brother to resume his dress.

The M∴ C∴ will lead the candidate out and return as soon as possible, present him to the 1st Surv∴ who will cause him to reach as a Fellow Craft as far as the altar. The M∴ R∴ M∴ then applies the point of the Compasses to the Candidate's breast, giving five raps upon the point with his gavel, saying:

M. R. M.—Learn so to control the feelings of your heart, and restrain the evil passions as to be most hurtful to mankind and to yourself.

Extending the sword over his head, says :

In the name of the G∴ A∴ O∴ T∴ U∴, under authority of the Supreme Council of the Ancient and Accepted Scotch Rite of Freemasonry, in and for the Sovereign and Independent State of Louisiana, and by virtue of powers on me conferred, I do hereby make and constitute you a Master Mason, and declare you an active member of the R∴ Lodge, (name and number.)

The M∴ R∴ M∴ then gives seven raps with his gavel upon the blade of his sword, and resumes his seat.

M. R. M.—Bro∴ M∴ C∴, please conduct brother (name,)

to the East for secret instructions.

The M∴ C∴ gives the candidate a seat near the 2d Surv∴, and the M∴ R∴ M∴ standing near, says :

M. R. M.—When you wish to enter a *Master Mason's* Lodge you must rap thus, (*shows him.*) The Inside Sentinel will return the rap, open the wicket and ask you the " word of pass" which you will divide with him thus, (*tells him the word and how to give it.*) When admitted you will approach the altar on these steps, (*shows him how to execute the Master's steps.*) They indicate the respect due to graves. You will then give the *Master's* sign to the East thus, (*shows him*;) face to the left and repeat to the 1st Surv∴, face about to the right and give the same sign to the 2d Surv∴ and take a seat near to the balustrade.

The grip was given with the five points of perfection.

The sign of distress must be given only in case of extreme peril ; this is it, (*shows him.*)

The battery is given thus, and your age as a *Master* ...... years. When asked by a competent person "If you are a Master Mason ?"—you will answer,—" the ...... is known to me."

The Compasses and the carpenter's plane are implements peculiar to this degree. The plane indicates to the accomplished workman that constant efforts are required in removing the asperities of life, that he may be the better prepared to reciprocate the amenities of social and professional intercourse, thereby reflecting honor upon himself and upon his fraternal associates.

Bro∴ M∴ C∴, please conduct Brother, (name,) to the West for examination in our secret instructions.

The 1st Surv∴ examines the candidate regarding the sign, words, grip and steps.

1st Surv.—M∴ R∴ M∴, the instructions are correct.

M. R. M.—Bro∴ M∴ C∴, please give Bro∴—— a seat in the East, and make the usual proclamation.

M. C.—Be it known to all within the Union Cord, that Bro∴ has been raised to the Master Mason's degree in accordance with the customs and statutes of the Ancient and Accepted Scotch Rite of Freemasonry, and admitted as an active member of the R∴ Lodge, (name and number,) in the city of .... under the authority of the Supreme Council of the Sovereign Grand Inspectors General of the 33d Degree, for the State of Louisiana, and the Fraternity is invited to receive and protect him accordingly.

The concluding ceremonies are similar to those in the preceeding degrees. Each degree has its peculiar sign and battery. The Lodge must be closed in the 3d, then in the 2d and finally in the 1st Degree.

LECTURE ON THE THIRD DEGREE.

M. R. M.—M∴ Ven∴ Bro∴ 1st Surv∴, are you a Master Mason?

M. V. 1st Surv.—M∴ Resp∴ M∴, I am, try me, the Acacia is known to me.

Q.—What does the Acacia symbolize?

A.—The Acacia by its nature is a symbol of Freemasonry; as a vood it is incorruptible;—by its bark, it presents an impenetrable shield to all mischievous insects, and by its leaves, which inclosed during the night and before sun rising, are again opened whilst the sun comes nearer to Zenith.

So with Freemasonry. It cannot be perverted by preposterous innovations; it offers an indestructible barrier to intolerance, fanaticism and tyranny; and its disciples, blindfolded in the first degree, come nearer to the great light, whilst they proceed to the Eighteenth and Thirtieth Degrees.

Q.—Where were you initiated to the Degree of Master Mason.

A.—In the Sanctum Sanctorum or Holy of Holies.

Q.—What did you see on entering?

A.—Mourning and consternation, in remembrance of a sad and calamitous event.

Q.—What was that event?

A.—The death of the Master, Hiram Abif, who had been murdered by three companions.

Q.—Is that murder a real and true fact?

A—It is viewed by Scotch Freemasons as a legend.

Q.—What is the meaning of such a fiction?

A.—Hiram Abif represents Justice and Truth; and the three companions, Jubela, Jubelo and Jubelum,—Ignorance, Hypocrisy and Ambition.

Q.—How were you then disposed of?

A.—Bro∴. Expert took me by a coffin and requested me to say whether I had participated in the death of the person, there lying.

Q.—What did you answer ?

A.—I answered, no.

Q.—What was the meaning of such a question, and of the sight offered to your eyes ?

A.—To impress on my mind that no man has the right to make an attempt upon the life of his fellow-beings, and that in the third degree mysteries of death should be fully illustrated and explained.

Q.—What next was made to you ?

A.—I had to make three voyages.

Q.—What is the philosophical or symbolic meaning of these three voyages ?

A.—That there are three distinct periods in the human life—Youth, Manhood and Senility. During the first period we are all apprentices and know very little ;—during the second, man becomes the companion of all reasonable beings, made by the Grand Architect of the Universe after his own image ;—and finally during the third, man is the great Master of Life, since he knows all its sufferings and pleasures, and being taught by experience he fully understands the necessity and reasons of death.

Q.—How were you disposed of after these three voyages ?

A.—I was requested to take the solemn obligation of the Master Mason.

Q.—Can you give me a proof that you remember your promise ?

A.—I can, by giving you the sign of the Third Degree.

Q.—Give it.

Q.—(He gives the sign.)

Q.—What does it mean ?

A.—That I should rather have my body severed in two than to violate the promise I made not only to keep silent about all secrets of the Third Degree, but also never to harm or injure the wife, daughter, sister or mother of a brother Mason.

Q.—Do you know another sign ?

12

A.—I do.

Q.—What is it?

A.—The sign of horror, which was made when the pall, thrown over the corpse of Hiram Abif, was taken away.

Q.—Make it.

A·—(The sign is made.)

Q.—What is the pass word of the Third Degree?

A.—(The pass word is given.)

Q.—What is the sacred word?

A.—I am ready to give it in a proper way. I have first to give the five points of perfection.

Q.—What are the five points of perfection?

A.—Hand to Hand, to show that we are united as two brothers—Foot to Foot, to indicate that, whatever may be the distance separating two Freemasons, they are bound to run to the assistance of each other—Knee to Knee, to remember us that we have a common creed, the belief in a Grand Architect of the Universe, and furthermore, should we kneel before God, we never kneel as Freemasons in presence of any man—Breast to Breast, that we ought to bury in our bosom all secrets instructed to us by a brother—Left hand on the right shoulder, that it is our duty never to permit a brother to be slandered when absent, and that, on the contrary, we ought to defend and protect his reputation.

Q.—What is your age as a Master Mason?

A.—Seven years and more. Seven because that number is required to have a just and perfect Lodge; and more, because I am now familiar with all secrets and mysteries of the Ancient and Accepted Scotch Rite of Freemasonry.

Q.—Should your life be in a great danger what should you do?

A.—The sign of distress.

Q.—Give it.

Q.—The sign of distress is given with the words "To me, the Widow's sons!"

FUNERAL SERVICE.

Lodge room hung in black, skulls, cross bones, tears, flowers, etc.

Coffin in the centre. If he was a Master the feet are turned to the South; if a R.˙. † feet are to the West. His jewels, apron and tools are placed symmetrically on the Coffin.

EMBLEMS ON THE CENOTAPH.

1. All seeing eye, surrounded by a serpent; 2. Skull from which butterfly seems to take its flight, 3. A reversed torch held by an Angel.

OTHER EMBLEMS.

1. A tripod of burning flame; 2. A basket of flowers; 3. The banner of the Lodge, hung or covered with crape.

OTHER EMBLEMS ON THE ALTAR.

1. A pot of incense; 2. Vase of water; 3. Vase of wine; 4. Vase of milk.

CEREMONIES.

The Ven.˙. M.˙. opens the Lodge in the usual form, except the Battery which is muffled and accompanied by the words—Mourn! Mourn! Mourn!

The visitors are then admitted. The Ven.·. M.·. pronounces a discourse relative to the occasion, the ceremony and the merits of the deceased.

Ven. M.—Bro·. 1st Surv.·., where is our Brother N ?

A.—He wanders in darkness.

M.—Can we withdraw him from that darkness?

A —The regions to which he has gone are unknown to us.

M.—Will he not be restored to light?

A.—The Grand Architect of the Universe towards whom his soul has taken its flight, and by whom alone it is guided, will lead him to the Temple of eternal Light and Truth.

M.—What is our duty towards the mortal remains of our Brother ?

A. —His body is due to the earth, from which it was taken, and unto the earth, passively and reverently, must we restore it, confiding in the wisdom and mercy of the G.·. A.·.

M.—Have we then lost our Brother forever?

A.—His visible body leaves us, but his name, his memory and his mind will be with us, time without end.

M.—Bro·. Secretary, inscribe on the record of this R.·. Lodge that on the———day of ———A. D.———N.·. returned unto his Creator, and that with due respect his brothers have consigned his body to the grave.

M.—Bro·. 1st Surv.·., what marks of honor do we owe our deceased Brother before consigning his body to the grave ?

A.—The symbols of Faith in his regeneration, which are the flowers we place on the altar.

The symbol of Strength by the libation of Wine.

The symbol of Truth and Purity by the Water of Purification.

The symbol of Love or Amity by the offering of Milk.

The symbol of Memorial Piety by burning Incense on the Altar.

M.—(! ! !...and all the BB.·. rise. Let us pray.

Oh ! Thou, Grand Architect of the U.·., light of life, in Thee do all things live and move and have their being. Material light and darkness unto Thee are alike, for Thou knowest not only the secrets of life, but also those of death. We rely on Thy infinite and eternal presence. May our Bro∴ N∴ be with Thee as he was with us, and may his death teach us to prepare ourselves to join him in the midst of the host of immortal souls which dwell with Thee and behold Thy face. Amen Amen! Amen!

Ven∴ M∴ descends, and after lighting the flame in the tripod, says: Sovereign Arbiter of Nature, Thou hast, in Thy wisdom, caused the end on earth of our brother, and Thou hast put a term to all of his misfortunes and sufferings. Thou hast delivered him from oppression and hast consoled his virtue. Thine infinite power and wisdom hath disposed all things so that nothing doth perish, and so that our souls cannot be annihilated any more than the matter in which they dwell on earth. We thank Thee, fervently, for the conscientiousness of the great and consoling truth which Thou hast made so evident, that we may calmly see the approach of death, and hope while we look upon this Coffin.

The Ven∴ M∴ takes a candle, and says:

Bro∴ N∴, thy brethren call thee, answer us !

(After the call the Ven∴ M∴ extinguishes the light.) This is repeated several times.

M.—Our brother is deaf to our voices. As the flame of this candle he was full of life, and like unto it he gave forth light among us, but a breath has extinguished it, and his light has gone to the source of all thought. In vain do we call him. Let us, therefore, proceed to render a final homage unto our brother, and may he, in the regions where now he dwells, be aware of our affectionate sentiments and sorrowing accents.

Master and Officers cast flowers on the Coffin, and Master says :

Though the sombre emblems of death hang upon these walls and surround this Coffin, though we weep, this departed brother and behold the decomposition of his body, let these flowers, which we cast upon his grave, remind us that in the bosom of destruction regeneration begins, that from death springeth life anew; that life is but a journey in the midst of eternity; and he who hath lived well has nothing to fear.

Master and Officers make libation of Wine, and Master says :

May the strength which sprung unto form and body, out of vegetable matter, follow and return with our brother unto the Grand Architect of the Universe, and continue to serve the purposes of omnipotence.

Master and Officers pour out Water, and Master says:

May truth of spirit and purity of conscience justify this brother before the all seeing eye, and may he stand approved by the Grand Architect who gave him this body to serve the designs of infinite wisdom.

Master and Officers pour out Milk.

M.—May the kindness of heart, our departed brother displayed to all men, the charity of his life, give him a title to the boundless mercy and love of the father of all.

Master and Officers burn Incense.

M.—May the soul of our brother ascend to the throne of God as the sweet perfumes of this incense rise to this dome or roof, and may the Grand Architect receive him in the Grand Lodge of Heaven, where none but the just can be admitted.

M.—Brethren, the moment has arrived when we must follow our regretted brother to the last abode of the body, but dispair not, as do those who confound their existence with that of the beasts who perish in dissolution, for the mind of man, which is the image and breath of God himself, is one and indissoluble.

The procession is formed.

Arrived at the grave the Master or Orator makes an appropriate exhortation.

The Master closes the tomb while the brethren cast branches of Acacia or evergreen into it or upon it.

When the tomb has been closed the members return to the Lodge, and it is closed.

www.ingramcontent.com/pod-product-compliance
Lightning Source LLC
Chambersburg PA
CBHW020034030726
47499CB00007B/2416